Atxago, Bernardo.

D1626066

THE LONE WOMAN

BERNARDO ATXAGA, a Basque, was born in 1951. He published his first work at the age of twenty in an anthology of Basque writers. He has written plays, children's books, radio scripts and novels, including *Obabakoak*, which has been published in fourteen languages including English, and won several prizes. His last novel, *The Lone Man*, was described by Peter Millar in *The Times* as "a spellbinding, sympathetic odyssey into the mind of a former terrorist".

MARGARET JULL COSTA translated *Obabakoak* and *The Lone Man*. She is also translator of works by Javier Marías (including *A Heart so White* which won the Dublin International Impac Award), Carmen Martín Gaite and Arturo Pérez-Reverte. Her translation of Fernando Pessoa's *The Book of Disquiet* made her joint-winner of the Portuguese translation prize.

By the same author in English translation

OBABAKOAK
THE LONE MAN

Bernardo Atxaga

THE LONE WOMAN

*Translated from the Spanish
by Margaret Jull Costa*

THE HARVILL PRESS

LONDON

First published in Spain with the title *Esos cielos* by Ediciones B, Barcelona, 1996

First published in Great Britain in 1999 by The Harvill Press
2 Aztec Row, Berners Road, London N1 0PW

www.harvill-press.com

3 5 7 9 8 6 4 2

Copyright © Bernardo Atxaga and Ediciones B, S.A., 1996
English translation © Margaret Jull Costa, 1999

Bernardo Atxaga asserts the moral right to be
identified as the author of this work

A CIP catalogue record for this book
is available from the British Library

This edition has been translated with the financial assistance of the Spanish Dirección
General del Libro y Bibliotecas, Ministerio de Cultura

ISBN 1 86046 421 1 (hbk)
ISBN 1 86046 422 X (pbk)

Designed and typeset in Photina at
Libanus Press, Marlborough, Wiltshire

Printed and bound in Great Britain by Butler & Tanner Ltd
at Selwood Printing, Burgess Hill

CONDITIONS OF SALE

The Lone Woman

She was a woman of thirty-seven who had spent the last few years in prison. Slight and serious-looking, she was dressed neatly in clothes of a somewhat masculine cut; when she walked, she did so slowly, calmly; when she spoke, her voice was surprisingly husky; when she looked, her eyes seemed hard – two brown spheres that time had polished to a sombre gleam. After her release from prison, she had spent a terrible night, wandering the bars of Barcelona, and ending up sleeping with a man she had only just met. Then, the following morning, after more bars and more walking, she had decided to return to the city where she was born, Bilbao. Forty minutes later, she was standing outside one of the sets of automatic doors at the railway station.

The door sensed her presence and trembled slightly, as if the two glass leaves were about to part at any moment, and then, acting instead as a mirror – for she had stopped and was looking at herself – it reflected her own figure back at her in precise detail: the leather suitcase she was holding with both hands, her black tights and black moccasins, her suede jacket with the red AIDS ribbon pinned to the lapel, her white shirt, her cropped hair. She kept looking herself up and down, like a woman who has just got dressed and is uncertain about her appearance.

"Not bad," she said quietly, staring at her legs. After all those years inside, it was odd to see herself full-length. The mirrors in prison were rarely more than two feet high.

The door trembled again and two hefty young foreign

women, carrying rucksacks taller than themselves, emerged from the station and occupied the space where her image had been. They took a couple more steps and stood before her.

"Could you help me, please?" asked one of them, unfurling what appeared to be a plan of the city as abruptly as if she were opening an umbrella. There was something vaguely insolent about her tone of voice, reminiscent of fifteen-year-old school-kids in TV sitcoms.

"No, I can't," said the woman, without even looking at her. She was in no mood to start poring over the map of a city in which almost the only thing she knew was the prison. Besides, she despised tourists, especially tourists carrying rucksacks.

The abruptness of her reply startled the two young women, although, after the initial shock, their look of surprise became an exaggerated grimace. How could she treat them like that? Had she no manners? Why was she so aggressive?

"You stink of sweat. Why don't you go and have a shower?" thought the woman, shifting her suitcase to one hand and going in through the door. She didn't understand what the two foreign women shouted after her. The English she had learned in prison was good enough for her to be able to read and, to some extent, speak, but not enough to understand the insults of British or American tourists.

Once inside the building, she felt as if she were about to faint, as if her legs would give way beneath her if she continued walking towards the people milling about in the waiting rooms or by the ticket office. She hurriedly sought refuge in the area behind one of the shops, less crowded, emptier than the rest. Things were happening all around her, everywhere: a red light began to blink, a child bumped into the luggage cart and fell flat on its face on the floor, someone rushed past, their head turned to look back at the electronic departures board. And in moments of calm, when the general bustle died down, her eyes collided – like the child who had fallen flat on his face – with the glittering glass columns or the loud yellow or red plastic surfaces.

"So, you're leaving us. Well, congratulations. I mean it. From now on, you'll have all the electric light you want."

The inside of the station more than bore out the truth of those words addressed to her, just as she was about to leave prison, by Margarita, one of her cellmates. There were lights everywhere: in serried ranks across the ceiling and reflected on the paved floor, creating a brilliant atmosphere that affected everything in the building, from the magazines and books to the sweets in the sweetshop. It was in stark contrast to prison, of course, because there, in the cells and along the corridors, darkness predominated – a kind of grey dust that filtered through the air and drowned the feeble glow from light bulbs and fluorescent tubes.

She looked restlessly about her, at the pizzeria to her left towards the rear, then over at the area full of coffee shops, but she couldn't see the information office. It wasn't where she remembered it, opposite the ticket office. As for the departures board – which again was new to her – Bilbao was not amongst the destinations of those trains about to leave.

She compressed her lips and gave an irritated sigh. The station clock – a very sober, black and white Certina – said it was twenty past two in the afternoon. According to her wristwatch – which was also a Certina, a man's watch – it was two twenty-three. She regretted not having phoned the station that morning. She was used to the rigid prison timetable, to a life that passed, not like a river or a current in the sea, but like the little wheels in a clock, always turning on the same axis, never changing speed, so anything unusual, any uncertainty, made her feel uneasy. She must find out what her travel options were as soon as possible.

She picked up her suitcase again, this time in her left hand, and joined the group of passengers who were waiting in an area furnished with green plastic chairs. She spotted a young man in soldier's uniform, reading a sports paper. She went over to him and asked for his help. Could he tell her where she might find the timetables?

"Why don't you ask the computer?" the soldier said to her, pointing to a rectangular column. Halfway up the column was a window filled by a bright blue screen.

She put her suitcase down on the ground and struggled to follow the instructions. She could only get the machine to tell her about trains travelling to places near Barcelona or to cities like Paris, Zurich or Milan. She sighed again. This was beginning to get on her nerves.

"Do you need any help?"

The soldier had joined her at the computer. She told him that she couldn't find the timetable for trains to Bilbao.

"There isn't a train until eleven o'clock tonight," said the soldier, with a slightly flirtatious smile. When he saw the look of amazement on her face, his smile broadened and he spoke to her rather differently. "Is that too late for you?" he said. "You could spend the rest of the day in Barcelona."

She wasn't in a hurry to get anywhere, not even to Bilbao, and she was on the point of accepting the invitation that lay behind the soldier's words. After all, it was the first invitation, albeit only half-spoken, tentative, that she had had in a long time, at least from anyone of the opposite sex, and she needed all the help she could to bolster her self-confidence; she needed to be looked at, spoken to, desired, as if she were a normal woman, not a whore – the role she had passively undertaken on her first night out of prison. However, barely twenty-four hours had passed since she left prison, and still less, only about ten hours, since her encounter with the stranger with whom she had gone to bed in a cheap hotel, and she felt like being alone. She looked at the soldier and declined his offer. She couldn't stay in Barcelona, she had to get to Bilbao as soon as possible.

"I'll tell you what then," said the soldier with a sigh. He was rather disappointed. "The best thing would be to go by bus. It leaves at about half past three and goes straight there on the motorway. You'll be home by ten o'clock tonight."

"You seem to know a lot about timetables," she said, forcing a smile.

"I've got a friend back in the barracks. He always gets that bus. He usually buys his ticket over there, behind the station. The company's called Babitrans."

The soldier said goodbye to her, joking about lost opportunities and sketching a military salute. For a moment, she thought of continuing the joke and adding a further thread to the relationship that had grown up between them, but, instead, she simply watched him walk away.

The soldier disappeared amongst the crowd, down the escalator that connected the station with the metro. Yes, it was a bit of bad luck not to have met him ten or twelve hours earlier. Or perhaps the real bad luck lay in having met the other man, the awful guy who had picked her up in a bar, the fourth or fifth that she had visited that night.

She noticed the cigarette machine next to the entrance to the pizzeria, and the thoughts going round in her head immediately changed direction and flew off to the period in her life when she could choose any brand of cigarette she liked or, rather, choose the brand with which she identified and which she would carry with her, at least on certain occasions, like an amulet. She felt suddenly happier and thought that her recovery could begin right there, with that trifling realization, her recovery of herself through the objects that had surrounded her in her previous life.

"Try to find your own things," Margarita had advised her when she said goodbye. "They wait for us and they are the only things that can help us when we get out of prison. When you leave here, try to remember what they were and set about finding them. They'll help you a lot. I'll do the same some day. I'll go back to Argentina and I won't stop until I find my knee-high leather boots."

The laughter with which her cellmate had closed that brief conversation floated in her head as she went over to the cigarette machine. Margarita was over sixty and still had a long prison sentence to complete. It was highly unlikely that she would ever return to her native Argentina.

Her favourite brand, Lark, was in the last column in the machine. She put three coins in the slot and pressed the button.

"At last!" she exclaimed to herself.

She hadn't been able to smoke that brand, her usual one, for several years; it was a brand she had chosen as an adolescent, as an emblem almost of her own personality. She had been "the girl who smoked Lark" and now, after spending four years in a prison cell in Barcelona, there was a chance of being that girl again. On the other hand, the maroon packet – an extremely rare sight inside the prison walls – proved to her that she really was out, that before too long she would have a new handbag, and in that handbag a key, the key to her own house, the object that best characterized those who were free.

She placed the packet on her open palm.

"Lark has an inner chamber of charcoal granules to smooth

the taste," she read. Above the letters, there was a cross-section of the filter showing the granules.

She put the pack in her jacket pocket and crossed over to the other part of the station via a side passage. Even before she reached the exit, she spotted two buses parked on the station forecourt; the first was white, the second yellow and white, and she had the impression that both had their engines running and were about to leave. She quickened her step and almost ran through the automatic doors at the end of the passage.

Startled by her sudden appearance, about a dozen sparrows took flight – up until that moment they had been pecking at the breadcrumbs scattered for them by an old woman.

"Where are you off to in such a hurry?" the old woman shouted in a disagreeable voice, before cursing the gusty wind snatching at her coat. She seemed slightly crazy.

The sparrows circled, flying into the wind, over the station in the direction of the prison, which was less than five hundred yards away from there. An idea flitted through her mind and made her smile. Those birds probably had their nests in holes in the prison walls. Indeed, that particular flock of sparrows were probably the ones she used to see from the tiny kitchen window or from the courtyard.

Two drivers were standing chatting by the yellow and white bus.

"Yes, this is the bus. It leaves at three forty and flies straight to Bilbao," said one of them. Both he and his colleague seemed in a good mood.

"Well, it flies when I'm driving. When you're driving, it crawls," added the second driver, and the two men burst out laughing and punched each other on the arm.

She looked at the clock. There was less than an hour before it left.

"Where do I buy a ticket?" she asked.

"In the station. Right over there," replied the driver who had made the joke, pointing to door number seven. "But you don't have to do that. My colleague here will be delighted to do it for you, won't you? He's very well brought up and a bit of a ladies' man too."

"Thanks, that won't be necessary," she said, forestalling the other driver's response. Then, simply in order to escape from them, she went and sat on a stone bench.

She put her suitcase down on the ground and took out the packet of cigarettes. The gold band from the cellophane wrapping and the silver paper covering the cigarettes flew off in the same direction as the sparrows, towards the prison.

And the smoke? Would that fly in the same direction too? She lit the cigarette with a plastic lighter, inhaled the smoke and then, suppressing all the memories that the taste of the tobacco evoked – memories of a school dance, memories of a day at the beach – she slowly exhaled. Just like the birds and the wrapping, the smoke headed off towards the prison.

She closed her eyes and shook her head. She must stop playing these games, she must keep calm and try to control the thoughts buzzing around in her head like a swarm of bees, only to end up always in the same place: prison.

"I have to move on. I'm out now," she murmured to herself. Nevertheless, she knew perfectly well that it was going to be very difficult to forget about prison. As difficult as it would be to give up the habits she had acquired there: talking to herself, for example.

She leaned back on the bench, and for the first time that day, she looked up at the sky. It wasn't a particularly pleasant sight. The sky was nothing like the "slow blue river" mentioned in a poem dedicated to Barcelona. On the contrary, it seemed to be made out of grey marble, like the top of a tomb. No, looking at the sky didn't help her much either. It was almost better to go on thinking about things that had happened in prison. Things which, in fact, were not things but people like Margarita or Antonia, her cellmates, her friends. She would have to keep her promise to write to them every fortnight or every month, and to send them books, and the odd picture to put up in their cell.

She finished her cigarette and, picking up her suitcase again, she went into the station. At first, as she walked towards the automatic doors, the faces of her two friends, Margarita and Antonia, remained in her mind, motionless, like two picture postcards; then, when she reached the bus-company office and stood in the queue, the image of Margarita came alive and the memory of her last day in prison reasserted itself.

"This is my present, for you to put in your house, in your bedroom," Margarita was saying to her as she moved about the cell, the scene of that particular memory. She was handing her a small picture, a detail from the fresco painted by Michelangelo in the Sistine Chapel: God and Adam reaching out to each other.

"I can't possibly accept it, I can't," she said, pushing it away. She knew how important that picture was to Margarita. On the nights when they would sit philosophizing, for example, when they had managed to get hold of a couple of beers and could allow themselves the luxury of staying up until the small hours talking and drinking, Margarita always ended up discussing that picture. There was one particular detail that had great significance for her – the gap between the two fingers. Despite all the efforts of both God and Adam, their fingers never touched. There was only a tiny space between them, but they didn't touch. What did that mean? The impossibility of man ever making contact with God? The impossibility of being good? Adam's independence from God his creator?

11

"You have to accept it, you must."

Margarita closed her eyes, adopting one of her favourite poses, that of a medium who has just gone into a trance, a pose that had given her quite a reputation amongst the women in prison; many thought she was mad, but, amongst those who were impressed by the way she spoke and by her evident culture, she had a reputation as a kind of priestess, a seer.

"Well, I'm not going to," she replied, rearranging the things she had already packed in her suitcase.

"I know how much you like the picture, almost as much as I do. I don't know why you like it, but you do. And the oddest thing of all is that you've never said so, you've kept the attraction it holds for you a secret. And that, as an Argentinian psychoanalyst would say, suggests the presence of something very important. Don't laugh, please. I'm convinced that the picture reminds you of something in your past life, something so important that you've never been able to tell anyone about it, not even after a few beers."

"What's even odder is that you've never found out," she said, no longer laughing.

"What does that scene remind you of?" Margarita insisted, taking the picture back and examining it closely. "You ought to tell me. You can't leave without at least giving me that satisfaction."

"It's nothing very special. It just reminds me of a boy I grew up with. He was a draughtsman and he was always talking to me about Michelangelo. That's all I can tell you, there's nothing more to it."

"I don't think you're telling the truth," said Margarita, looking her in the eye.

"You're quite right, but you were so insistent that you forced me to invent something," she confessed, holding her gaze. She

12

was getting a bit impatient. She wanted to finish packing.

"So I was right; it is something important!" exclaimed Margarita. "I knew it all along. People always hide the really important things."

Although the rumours circulating in prison spoke of the kidnapping of a child, no one knew exactly why Margarita had been given such a long sentence. That was her secret, the thing that she would never talk about, not even on those rare nights when they all got slightly drunk.

"Anyway, the picture is yours. You're to pack it in your suitcase."

"All right, if you insist."

Margarita placed the picture amongst the clothes and the books.

"What books are you taking with you?"

Before she had time to reply, Antonia, their other cellmate, appeared. She was a young woman of about thirty, though she looked older, the consequence of the life she had led before she was sent to prison.

"You are a mean sod, leaving us just when we were having a good time. You're heartless, you are," she said as soon as she came in, underlining her reproach with a little shove.

"And that's not the worst of it, she's taking with her the entire contents of number eleven," Margarita added, rummaging around in the suitcase and taking out one of the books that had just been packed. "Number eleven" was a cell fitted out as a library, a victory for the inmates on their corridor.

"I've only taken my favourite books, about ten of them. And they're nearly all duplicates."

"So Stendhal is amongst the chosen few," said Margarita, opening the copy of *Scarlet and Black* that she had in her hands. "I don't know if I would choose that. No, I don't think I would."

She put the book down and peeked again in the suitcase.

"And what about your English books? Have you got those too?"

"Yes, teacher, I've got them too."

Antonia followed Margarita's lead and took another of the books out of the suitcase. It was an anthology of poetry.

"Here's our poem," said Antonia, turning to a particular page. And she started reading out loud.

> Beat at the bars.
> Cry out your cry of want.
> Let yourself out if you can.
> Find the sea, find the moon,
>   if you can.

"I hate that poem. Stop it," Margarita said, interrupting her. She snatched the book from her hands and returned it to the suitcase.

There were certain things, like cigarettes, alcohol or barbiturates, that helped to make imprisonment bearable. However, it was reading that had helped her most, or, to be more precise, the little literary group that Margarita, Antonia and she had formed around cell number eleven, an island inside the prison, a place which, as well as functioning as a library, occasionally served as a lecture hall. According to Margarita's calculations, about ninety per cent of the prisoners had been in that cell at some time, but only about fifteen could be said to be regulars.

"Have you gone to sleep?" she heard someone say. The man at the ticket office was staring at her from the other side of the counter. He was a very spruce young man, with his hair slicked back. He seemed impatient.

She apologized and asked for a ticket to Bilbao. In the smoking section.

"I don't want to poke my nose in, but, if I was you, I wouldn't travel in the smoking section," said the young man, talking very fast.

"Look, just give me the ticket," she insisted. She had a deep dislike of hysterical people.

"Now calm down, don't get angry. Let me explain," the young man said, still gabbling. "The thing is, our buses are double-deckers, and the lower deck, which is reserved for smokers, isn't even half as big as the top deck. And if there are a lot of passengers," the young man went on, talking quickly so that she wouldn't interrupt him, "all the smokers travelling on the top deck come downstairs whenever they feel like a smoke and a real fug builds up. Do you see what I mean?"

"You've convinced me," she said. She didn't want to prolong the conversation.

"Seat number thirty-two," said the young man, holding the ticket out to her. "And I'm sorry if I poked my nose in where it wasn't wanted."

"It doesn't matter."

"Do you know why I gave you that advice? Because I've often travelled downstairs myself. We employees have to. They make us sit downstairs even if there are free seats on the top deck. I get sick every time I have to make a trip."

"Why don't you protest?" she said, addressing him now as "tú" and raising her voice a little. "Call a strike. And if the company won't give in, steal a bus and burn it."

"Right," said the young man, with a nervous smile.

"I've got forty-five minutes before the bus goes. Where can I eat around here?"

"There's a self-service restaurant next to the left luggage. It's called the Baviera. That's the best place. As for what I was saying about the bus, it's no big deal. We're all quite happy with the company really."

The young man looked away. He regretted ever having started that conversation.

The Baviera was an impersonal place, all plastic and steel, protected from the noise of the station by great glass screens. She liked it, mainly because it was quiet, thanks to the screens and the absence of any piped music. She was starting to get a headache and the silence made the air grow fresher again, or so it seemed.

Leaving her case in the corner farthest from the entrance, she went up to the counter and chose two dishes: a salad of mussels and green peppers, and pasta in tomato sauce.

"Have you got any small bottles of vermouth?" she asked the waitress at the hot-meals counter.

"Only what you can see," the waitress replied, pointing to a tray packed with bottles and cans of drink.

She placed two cans of beer between the two plates of food and went over to the checkout. Then, returning to her table, she sat down in a chair from which she could see the whole place and took a good look at all the customers: diagonally opposite, at the other end of the restaurant, there was a man, apparently a foreigner, eating alone; nearer to her, taking up three tables, there were about ten young men with very short hair – soldiers out of uniform probably – eating sandwiches and telling jokes; then there was a table occupied by a boy and a blind man wearing dark glasses; then there was her, in perfect symmetry with the foreigner at the other end – with no friends to talk to, no travelling companions.

She felt tired. Her headache was becoming more intense above one eye.

"I'm really spaced out," she thought, staring at the foreigner at the opposite end. She had no one to talk to. No one had been waiting for her outside the prison. No one was waiting for her in Bilbao. As Antonia or Margarita would have said, she didn't have much going for her, only about as much as some wretched tourist in a strange country.

She shook her head – which made it hurt a little more – and tried to banish the ideas surfacing in her mind. Pity was a vile emotion, and self-pity was even worse, the vilest emotion of all. She must keep an eye on herself, be severe with herself. In her situation, normal behaviour – the behaviour of someone who has never been in prison – wasn't enough. One of the poems she had read in the library in cell number eleven said: "I never saw a wild thing sorry for itself. A small bird will drop frozen dead from a bough without ever having felt sorry for itself." It was true, and she could be no less than the sparrows she had frightened away near the buses on the forecourt.

The mussels that came with the salad reminded her of the tins that Antonia, Margarita and she used to eat in the pantry at the far end of the kitchen, a place which they called the sanctum sanctorum, because it was the focus of those private celebrations. Generally, it would just be the three of them. According to Margarita, it was the ideal number of guests.

"Three people can eat together really well; they can eat and keep up a flow of conversation at the same time. Four, on the other hand, is disastrous. The conversations keep cutting across each other."

"What about two? How does that work?"

"Sometimes it can work really well with two, Antonia. But, in my experience, it's better to eat alone than in company."

But in order to feel comfortable alone at her table – her thoughts were following the thread of her memory – it would be best to have something to read, and she didn't even have a newspaper. During that morning, it had occurred to her to buy a newspaper from the Basque country, but in the end she hadn't felt like it and so hadn't done so. As for the books she had in her suitcase, she didn't want to risk getting food on them. Besides, they weren't the sort of book you could read during a meal.

Then she remembered the letter. She had written it after breakfast in a café in Las Ramblas, and it was still in her inside jacket pocket. Why not? She could read it again and decide once and for all whether or not she should send it. And if she got food on it? In that case, she would interpret the stain as a bad omen and she would tear the letter up.

She pushed away the now empty plate of mussels and wiped the edge of the table with a paper serviette. Then she opened the second can of beer, took the letter out of the envelope and started to read what she had written. What did she really want? Did she want some of the pasta to slip off her fork and on to the paper? Did she want to withdraw what she had said? She didn't know, she couldn't know until she had read the letter through from start to finish.

> Andoni,
>
> At last I'm out of that hole of a prison and I think the moment has come to clarify a few things. I don't love you and you don't love me, so, as my cellmate, Antonia, used to say: fuck off. I don't want to see you ever again, and the only thing I regret is that it's taken me so long to get round to saying it. I should have told you to fuck off ages ago, not now. Because you've been a lousy friend, a bad friend who abandoned me whenever I had a problem and only ever gave me bad advice. When I started sorting out my paper-work in prison, for example, what did you say? You told me to wait, to be careful, to consult the organization hierarchy.

Hearing you talk, anyone would think you were a serious militant counselling a less serious one and yet – oh, fuck off, Andoni, fuck off – you've never been a politically active member of anything, not even a club for foodies. If you had been a true friend, you would never have talked to me like that, because, at least in my experience, being fond of someone usually makes you selfish, selfish enough to think only of yourself and your loved ones, not about what would suit the organization or what those who are above good and evil might advise.You should have said to me, yes, leave prison, it doesn't matter if the others accuse you of being a traitor, I'll support you, we'll go on a trip, I'm longing to be with you. But that isn't what you did. You did exactly the opposite.

Obviously, you won't agree.You'll say what you used to say when you came to see me, that you need me, and I agree, what you need is a big sack that you can empty all your sorrows and your bad news into, but I'm not going to be that sack any longer, you can find another one. Come to think of it, you'd be an awful friend to have for everyday use. You're so mean, so petty!

By now, Andoni, you'll be wondering why I'm writing you this letter, since I seem to feel such hatred for you all of a sudden, because I think that's precisely what it is, hatred; the more I write, the more clearly I see that. I mean, it's not just what I said at the start, about me not loving you and all the rest, it's worse than that, it's quite simply that I hate you. Especially after what happened tonight. Do you know what I did? I went to bed with a man I didn't even know. It was utterly humiliating. He treated me like a whore, though I was much cheaper than any whore, because I paid for almost all the beers. And the hotel he took me to must

19

have been the cheapest in Barcelona, even the sheets were dirty. Do you know what I think? I think it's all your fault. If you had been a better friend, if I had found you waiting for me outside prison, none of that would have happened.

Anyway, like I said, Andoni: fuck off. And don't even attempt to contact me in Bilbao. If you do, you'll be sorry.

Should she send the letter, or tear it up? She lit a cigarette and started analysing her feelings with the subtlety of someone trying to understand the inner meaning of each and every ripple on the surface of a river. She still couldn't find a precise answer, though. On the one hand, it was clear that the letter was born of a particular state of mind, her state of mind that morning following her ghastly sexual encounter with the man who had picked her up in a bar; besides, it was unfair, even unnecessarily cruel, the letter omitted anything that might give a more balanced view of events, for example, the financial help that Andoni had given her during those years; on the other hand, the reproach that lay at the heart of what she had written – the lack of joy in their relationship – exactly reflected a feeling that had been growing day by day long before she fell into the hands of the police.

She inhaled the smoke from her cigarette and looked around her. The foreigner at the table opposite was no longer alone, now he was accompanied by a woman and by a girl of about ten. And the group of soldiers out of uniform had grown too and now spilled over onto two more tables. At the table near her, the boy sitting next to the blind man was eagerly examining the tickets, as if doing so gave him pleasure.

"Great," he said to the blind man, putting the tickets away, "we'll be home before eight."

"What are you going to make me for supper? I'm fed up with

this Barcelona rubbish," said the blind man with a broad smile. He too seemed content.

"I'll make you a huge potato omelette. How would that suit you?"

"Fantastic," said the blind man emphatically.

The person whom she had taken for a boy was, in fact, a very short woman. However – as the message being given out by her surroundings made crystal clear – she was the only person on her own in the restaurant. Years ago, whenever she came back from a school trip or from a holiday, she would find her parents and her brothers at the station, and if her family couldn't be there, then her friends would meet her. Now, after four years in prison, she had no one.

She stubbed the cigarette out on the floor and put the letter back in its envelope. Her thoughts had changed in tone and had become aggressive. Why had no one come to meet her? Where were her brothers? And what about her friends? She knew that many of them despised her for leaving the organization and taking on the role of reformed terrorist, but she found it hard to believe that everyone felt like that, that all her friends from before felt like that, without exception. And Andoni? But she could expect nothing from him. He had turned out to be a weak man, a puppet incapable of rejecting the prevailing ethos of the places he frequented. "You've been a lousy friend, a bad friend who abandoned me whenever I had a problem," said her letter, and it was true.

With her suitcase in one hand and the letter in the other, she left the self-service restaurant and hurried over to where she remembered seeing a postbox. The thoughts that had just gone through her head had made her furious: her family, her friends, society itself – which was no more than an extension of the family – had been a refuge during her childhood, a kind

of carpet she could safely cross, without touching the icy floor, without hurting herself, as the poem said, on the sharp stones of the labyrinth; but then, as a person grew and matured, that carpet began to wear thin, to unravel, or worse still, to become viscous, a sticky coating that stuck to your feet and stopped you moving. And woe to anyone who rebelled against that viscous substance! Woe to anyone who renounced the law of the family!

> No, people never like
> those who keep their own faith.

No, people didn't like you having your own opinions, they would set themselves up as judges, judges who judged and always condemned. Because that was one of the characteristics of puppets, their judgments always, inevitably, turned into condemnations. That is how they had behaved towards her. And still did. They had made her life impossible, first, because she had gone to live with her boyfriend, then, because, despite having married him, she had decided not to have children, and later, because she had got divorced; later still, it had been her involvement in politics and, lastly, her decision to leave the organization and get out of prison. Again and again, with every major decision she took, she found herself surrounded by that sticky substance secreted by those around her, decent, altruistic people all of them, all wanting to set her on the right path.

"Fuck off, Andoni," she murmured as she posted the letter. At that moment, her friend's name denoted a much wider territory.

The clock on the main wall of the station said three twenty. She rejected the idea of buying a Basque newspaper and, feeling calmer, relieved to have got rid of that letter, she went to the toilets next to the entrance to the metro. She would go to the toilet and then out to where the buses were. Although the atmosphere in the station was beginning to seem attractive to her – an intermediate landscape between prison and the outside world – her headache was getting worse and she needed some fresh air.

"I'm eighteen," she read on the toilet door, while she was peeing, "and I'd like to get in touch with girls my own age. If you're interested, just hang around here any Saturday at 7 p.m. Wear a white hat, just to make sure."

It wasn't the only message. The door was more like a small ads page. And there was no shortage of obscenities either, some even in verse:

> I like my women
> on their backs in their beds
> with no knickers on
> and their skirts over their heads.

When she came out of the toilet she saw a line of light-green telephones. She stopped in front of one, put her suitcase down on the ground and felt around in her jacket pockets. She put two hundred-peseta coins in the machine and dialled a number.

"Hello, Dad," she said when she got through.

There was a silence at the other end.

"You're out then," said a voice grown feeble with the years.

"I'll be home tonight. How are you?"

"Fine," said the voice. Then there was a sob. Trying to get a grip on himself, he asked: "How are you getting here?"

"On the bus."

She had to bite her bottom lip. Despite herself, she too felt like crying.

"I'll call your brothers. I'll tell them to pick you up at the bus station."

"No, don't tell them anything, Dad. I'll either get a taxi or I'll walk. Really, Dad, I'd prefer it like that."

"I see. What you mean is that those people will be there to meet you with their flags and their noise," said the voice.

"No, it's not that."

"You shouldn't mix with people like that. I've told you before . . ."

"Dad, please," she said firmly, though without raising her voice. The numbers on the little screen on the telephone were beginning to blink. Her money was running out. "Honestly, no one's going to be there to meet me. Haven't they told you? I'm a traitor now."

"Your brothers hardly ever come here any more. And when they do, they don't say anything. That's what happens when you get old. No one . . ."

They were cut off. She swore and slammed down the receiver. It was always the same, always. Her good intentions never got her anywhere.

Annoyed by the failure of her phone conversation, she hurriedly left the station and went over to the buses. Before leaving the pavement and crossing the street, however, she stopped and decided to remain by the automatic doors until all the people crowding round the yellow and white bus had found their seats. She didn't feel like talking to anyone. She didn't want to run the risk of getting stuck with a talkative fellow passenger.

She took out a cigarette and looked up: the sky was still grey, but it had lost that hard look. It was no longer like a slab of marble, it was more like a dirty sheet, as dirty as the sheets on the bed she had slept in the night before.

She put her cigarette to her lips and started looking for her lighter.

24

"Allow me," she heard a voice say behind her. Startled, she stepped aside and spun round with her fists raised.

"Leave me alone!" she yelled at the man who had spoken to her, knocking the match out of his hand. The match fell to the ground, but it didn't go out.

"There's no need to be like that," said the man with a smile that seemed to well up from the very centre of his eyes. He was about her age and was wearing a well-cut brown suit with a red tie. He looked like a singer of romantic ballads.

"I said 'Leave me alone'," she said again, removing the cigarette from her lips.

"Can't we talk?" said the man, still smiling. He sounded very self-assured.

Panic suddenly gripped her. It was as if something – like a ball of cotton wool soaked in alcohol – had started to burn inside her, as if the stranger's match had set fire to all the fear that had accumulated there over those past few years; it was a cold fire, though, paralysing. While she was running for the bus, her heart began beating faster, and her memory repeated to her, again and again, thudding in her head, the lines that a colleague in the same organization had written after he had escaped from prison:

> The mind of an ex-prisoner
> Always returns to prison.
> In the street, he passes judges, prosecutors and lawyers,
> and the police, though they don't know him,
> look at him more than at anyone else,
> because his step is not calm or assured,
> because his step is far too assured.
> Inside him lives
> a man condemned for life.

Like the man in the poem, she too felt observed, scrutinized, persecuted, and she had the feeling that the eyes watching her were wrapping her in a sticky web that stifled her and trammelled her every movement. But as soon as she joined the queue of people getting on the bus, she faced up to her feelings of panic and – after retrieving the cigarette from her pocket and lighting it – managed to get her mind free from the weight of fear, to begin to analyse what was going on around her. What was really going on? Was she being observed? Was anyone actually looking at her? No, she had no reason to think that. There was no sign that she was being watched. The passengers nearest her were chatting in groups or pairs, and the taxi drivers parked nearby were listening to the radio or reading the newspaper. And what about the constant flow of people coming out of the station? And those who were sitting on the benches outside? No, they were all looking somewhere else, no one was paying her the slightest attention. And the man in the red tie? She didn't have to worry about that either. He hadn't followed her. He was nowhere to be seen.

At the door of the bus, a hostess was checking the passengers' tickets. The two drivers, who were still in the same mood they had been in an hour before, were trying to joke with her.

"You should get your hair cut short like this young lady," said one of them, winking at her.

"You're in seat thirty-two. Upstairs, almost directly above this door," said the hostess, frowning. She seemed fed up with the drivers' rudeness.

"Could I stay downstairs? I'm smoking," she said, showing her the cigarette. And she craned her neck and looked inside, where she saw a tiny counter with a coffee machine, and a sort of lounge area.

"Smoking's bad for you," said one of the drivers, the most talkative one.

"You can't come downstairs until the bus has set off. Just go to your seat, please."

The hostess' voice was as jarring to her as the attitude of the two drivers. The hostess had spoken to her in the severe tones of a prison warder.

"We'll put your suitcase away for you," said the talkative driver, holding out his hand.

"Can't I keep it with me? I want to look at some of the books I've got in there during the journey. Besides, it's not very big," she said, trying to be nice.

"If that's what you want. I never argue with a woman. Well, only with my wife," replied the driver, and he and his colleague burst out laughing.

A nun came running up from the far side of the bus depot; she was out of breath. She was about sixty and had come on ahead of her much older companion, who was walking towards them, taking short steps.

"Is this the bus to Bilbao?" the first nun asked the drivers.

"Have you got tickets?" asked one of the drivers, glancing over at the other nun who had not yet arrived.

"No," said the nun. She was a tall woman, with a rather Nordic air about her. She had green eyes.

"Well, you'd better buy them as soon as possible. You'd better run over to the ticket office. We're just about to leave."

"Running's very good for the health," added his colleague.

The nun's green eyes fixed on those of the second driver. At first, the man held her gaze, then lowered his eyes and mumbled an apology.

"Where is the ticket office?" asked the nun coldly, at the same time gesturing to her companion to stop where she was and wait.

"Go into the station through gate number seven and the office is right there," she told the nun, before the drivers or the hostess could say anything. Then she stubbed out her cigarette on the ground with her foot and got on the bus.

"I've got a great film for the video. Those two little nuns will just love it," said the driver as she was going up the steps. He sounded vengeful. He was feeling uncomfortable because, moments before, he had allowed himself to be intimidated by the nun.

Through the bus window, above the roofs crammed with aerials, the sky – the dirty sheet – had begun its transformation. Across one section of it there were five or six blue parallel lines, as if it really were a sheet and someone had been slashing at it with a knife. Weren't mattresses usually blue? Because what was up there was also blue. What's more – she closed her eyes when she noticed this – the clouds near those blue lines were tinged with red, the colour of a bloodstain that someone had tried and failed to wash out.

"You're not thinking of leaving, are you?"

In her memory she could only see certain parts of the body of the man asking her that question, his white hands, his hairy belly, his thick neck. They were in the cheap hotel room where they had spent the night; the man was on the bed and she was standing beside the wardrobe, getting dressed.

Yes, she said, she was.

"Well, you can forget that. I had too much to drink last night and I wasn't on form. I'm fine now though. Come back to bed. Now."

The man was scrutinizing her. His voice had a metallic edge to it.

"Now, do you hear! I don't like having to argue with whores!"

"There's no need to shout. Just give me time to light a cigarette."

She didn't know what the filter of a cigarette was made of, but, thanks to a self-defence course she had taken when she was a student, she did know that if you lit it and worked it into a point with your fingers it became a sharp weapon, like a bradawl made of black glass.

She retrieved her packet of cigarettes and took one out. They were Havanos, the only kind she could find in the dive where they had drunk their last beer the night before.

"You've lit the wrong end! I can smell it from here!" said the man, lying down on the bed.

"You're right," she replied while she sharpened the point. She burned her fingers slightly, but she felt no pain.

After a few seconds, she felt the base of the filter. The material had become completely crystallized. It now formed a sharp point. Holding the weapon between her index finger and her thumb, she hurled herself on the bed.

The man let out a howl when she lunged at him with the filter and drew a line across his belly; he tried to beat her off with his fists. But the two cuts that followed the first – in parallel, from his penis to his throat and from his throat back down to his penis – stopped him in his tracks. Maddened by pain, terrified by the blood pouring from his wounds and beginning to stain the sheets, he fled from the room, not out into the street, since he was naked, but to some other part of the hotel.

The nun with green eyes came out of the station and joined her companion before going up to the door of the bus. When she saw them, she stopped thinking about what had happened in the hotel and started thinking about those two women instead: where did they live? Sheltered from the misfortunes of the world, in some enclosed order? Or did they work in a hospice, with people suffering from terminal illnesses? In a way, she felt a certain kinship. All three had taken the difficult option. She had entered a radical political organization; the nuns, even if they were not from an enclosed order, had opted for the most testing section in their church.

Before she realized it, the bus had moved off. It made its way very slowly round the station, past a hotel and up a rather narrow street.

The woman read the street sign: "Carrer Nicaragua" and every nerve in her body tensed. The prison she had left the previous evening faced on to four streets, and that was one of them.

The bus reached a crossroads and turned towards the main prison gate, as if the driver wanted to show her the outside of a building which, despite the four years she had spent there, she knew only from inside. First, she looked up at the watchtower, at the guard with his blue and red beret, and then, shifting her gaze slightly to the left, she let her eyes linger on the grey roof of an annex to the main building. The women's section was housed under that grey roof, and the fourth window from the end belonged to the cell that Margarita, Antonia and she had shared or, rather, the cell that Margarita and Antonia continued to occupy. It was number seven. She remembered the song:

> If you want to write to me
> you know where I am,
> in cell number seven
> just waiting for a line.

A van parked opposite the main gate forced the bus to stop. Outside the prison, walking up and down the pavement or sitting on the kerb, the people who had gone to visit their relatives were growing bored with waiting and trying somehow or other to pass the time. They chatted, smoked, knitted, studied the wheels of the bus. They all looked rather ill. They were badly dressed, in cheap, ugly clothes. Most were women. Yes, the law was like a line drawn along the bottom of a mountain, and the people who were most exploited and had the fewest economic resources crossed that line as easily as a rubber ball bouncing down the mountainside.

The van drove inside the prison and the bus set off. She looked again at her cell window.

"Bye," she whispered, with the image of Margarita and Antonia in her mind. Although it was only a short word, it splintered in her throat, or, rather, deeper down than that, and she started to cry. She was crying silently, her eyes closed.

"Everything has a solution. Not even death is as terrible as it seems," said her neighbour in a friendly voice. She was a woman in her mid-fifties, and very heavily built. She must have weighed more than fifteen stone.

"How do you know?" she asked.

The bus was continuing up the street, following the blue signs to the motorway. It slipped along like a fish.

"I know because I've been very close to death myself. I've touched it with my fingertips you might say," replied the fat woman. She was speaking in a faint voice, as if she were half-asleep. "Don't worry, I'm not going to tell you the story of my life. It wouldn't be right. We all prefer to travel in silence, to have time to think about our own things, I mean."

"I don't object to people telling me their life story, but not right now. I'm going downstairs to have a cup of coffee."

"Yes, sometimes that can help too."

When she got up from the seat, she felt a sharp pain in her forehead; at least, her encounter with the man with the red tie had made her forget her headache. Nevertheless, that thought reawoke her fear and made her examine the people who were travelling on the upper deck, first those ahead of her, then – as she turned round to go down the stairs – those behind. She calmed down a bit when she saw that the man with the red tie wasn't there, but her fear kept asking questions. Did the police intend to follow her? She thought not, but given the appearance of two or three of the other passengers, and the rumours that had been going around prison – about the Anti-terrorist Brigade's interest in those who had been amnestied – she could not be sure.

"If you want to leave your case here, I'll look after it for you," said the fat woman.

"Thanks, but there are a few books inside that I want to look at."

"Yes, books can be very helpful too."

The bus driver accelerated as soon as he reached an avenue that led to the motorway. While she was going down the stairs, she noticed a blue line, right in the far distance, beyond the churches, the streets and the houses. It wasn't the sky, it was the sea.

Just as the young man at the bus company had warned her, the lower deck was much smaller than the upper deck. There was a dark plastic curtain separating off the area reserved for the driver, while the rear section, from the stairs to the back of the bus, seemed to be the luggage compartment. As for the remaining space, it was divided between a galley kitchen with a counter, a toilet, the small area reserved for smokers – which had a table with six seats around it – and the few seats reserved for actual passengers. The objects attached to the ceiling and the walls – the stainless steel sink or the coffee machine and, further along, the video screen – made the space seem even smaller.

That cramped area was occupied by only three people: the hostess and the two nuns.

"They haven't had much luck," she thought, looking over at the nuns and nodding to them. They had to travel in the smokers' section with a video screen immediately above them.

"Do you want anything?" asked the hostess adopting the same expression, irritable yet fawning, that she had worn when talking to the drivers. Was she really a hostess? She seemed more like a policewoman.

"A coffee, please, and a Bacardi with ice," she said. She put her case on the table in the smokers' section and sat down next to the window.

"We don't serve alcohol. The company . . . "

"Fine, bring me a coffee then." Again she felt that stab of pain in her head, this time on the left side.

She breathed deeply so as not to give in to her irritation with the hostess. She didn't want to spoil the journey, her first after four years of being locked up.

She took out a small key from her inside jacket pocket and opened the suitcase, thinking about the books she had packed. She wanted to have them near, to touch them, to open them at random and leaf through them. Now that she was out, they might not perhaps give her as much consolation as in prison, but she was sure that they would help her in what, to quote Margarita, was her "re-entry into the world", because, like Lazarus, she had been buried and, like him, she had been restored to life.

The picture that Margarita had given her – the image of God and Adam reaching out to each other – was on top of everything else in the suitcase and was the first thing she saw when she opened it. She placed it on the seat next to her and piled up six books on the table. There was a novel by

Stendhal – *Scarlet and Black* – an essay by Jorge Oteiza – *Quousque tandem* – the memoirs of Zavattini, an anthology of Chinese poems, a collection of Emily Dickinson's poems and Van Gogh's letters to his brother. When she had finished piling up the books, she made another pile with her notebooks.

She was just about to put the picture away again, when she realized that there was something written on the back. She read it slowly, trying to decipher what it said. It was a poem. A poem written in Italian.

Dalle più alte stelle
discende uno splendore
che'l desir tira a quelle
e che si chiama amore.

She looked up from the last word in the poem and glanced out of the window. As they left Barcelona behind them, a second city was emerging, its other half, its sinister underbelly. There, the ground on which the new, freshly painted buildings stood seemed scorched; the grey factories seemed exhausted, oppressed by the weight of the world. The hills, though, were green and pretty, crowded with houses, doubtless the refuge of the people in charge of the running of that second city.

The bus drove over the bridge linking two of those hills and she fixed her gaze on the muddy river flowing down below. The banks were full of seagulls which, oblivious to the roar of traffic, appeared to be scavenging for rubbish; there must have been about a hundred of them, possibly two hundred. One of them took flight and rose rapidly until it was lost against the sky. Over there, the sky was the same colour as the seagull, half grey and half white.

"You should leave your suitcase by your seat. Other passengers have a right to sit here too, you know," said the hostess, placing before her a tray with coffee, a spoon, a paper serviette and a sachet of sugar.

"I'm perfectly well aware of that. I know you're not supposed to leave suitcases on the table," she replied, picking up the plastic cup and placing it in one of the round holes in the table.

She put the picture back in the suitcase, closed the case and placed it on the floor.

"I didn't mean to offend you," said the hostess without a glimmer of emotion. "Do you want any headphones?" she asked, showing her a little red box.

"What are they for? For the film?"

"One of the channels is for the video. The others are for listening to music. Do you want them?"

She nodded and held out her hand for the red box.

"That's two hundred pesetas," said the hostess, seeing that she made no move to reach for her purse.

"I'm sorry. I thought they were included in the price of the ticket."

She took her purse out of her jacket pocket and held it very close to her chest as she opened it. She didn't want the hostess to know how little money she had. She only had one note and a few coins. And that was the worst thing – the idea came to her suddenly, like a revelation, the revelation of something that she already knew, but which she had relegated to a far corner of her mind – that this money was nearly all she had. Yes, money was going to be a problem. Because the real problem, the number one problem, the problem that encompassed all other problems, was always money. What ailed a madman was not his madness, but the fact that his madness stopped him earning any money. And the same could be said of someone who was ill or of someone like her, who had just got out of prison.

"Sorry, with the coffee that's three hundred," said the hostess, taking the coins she gave her, but keeping her hand open. She seemed tense.

She hurriedly gave her the extra money and the hostess smiled mechanically and disappeared behind the plastic curtain that separated the driver's area from the rest of the lower deck. Was she really an employee of the bus company? That suspicion – that fear – again opened up a path inside her, crept in through the interstices, like a current of air, and she felt suddenly afraid of finding herself in the middle of one of those stories people were always telling in prison, about the inmate who is released, but followed by the police and eventually picked up again, only to end up even worse off than before.

She relaxed her shoulders and lit a cigarette. She shouldn't be afraid. Regardless of whether the police were following her, regardless of whether her suspicions were correct, she had no reason to worry. She wasn't going to commit a crime. Nor was she going to become paranoid. The books would help her, her notebooks would help her. Just as they had in prison.

She picked up one of the notebooks that she had left on the table; it was the one containing her English exercises. She opened it at random and read a little poem that Margarita had used at the start of her classes to help her students – two prostitutes, as well as Antonia and herself – to memorize the names of the days of the week in English:

> Solomon Grundy
> born on Monday,
> christened on Tuesday,
> married on Wednesday,
> took ill on Thursday,
> worse on Friday,

died on Saturday,

buried on Sunday,

and that was the end of Solomon Grundy.

Outside, the landscape was gradually shrugging off the weight of the city and taking on its usual appearance: farm buildings, trees, birds. Three crows, sitting on a cable running parallel to the motorway, had turned their backs on the traffic and seemed absorbed in their thoughts. When she looked at them, the birds flew off.

"The life of Solomon Grundy was very short. Time flies like a bird. Time flies as the arrow does," she read, returning to the notebook.

Nothing existed in a pure state. That English notebook was not just an English notebook. It was also her diary and it perfectly reflected her different states of mind.

"Time is a wonderful thing. We must not use it up staying in prison."

She took a sip of coffee and then, with the pen that she kept in her jacket pocket, she crossed out a word and amended the phrase she had just read.

"Time is a wonderful thing. We must not waste it staying in prison," she read. That change seemed to her to improve the sentence.

She inhaled the smoke from her cigarette and read through some of the other things written in the notebook. She paused at a page full of numbers. It wasn't her writing, but Margarita's.

More memories surfaced in her mind.

"You've been here three years, ten months and twenty days. If you leave here next Tuesday, that will be a total of three years, ten months and twenty-seven days," Margarita had said to her, writing down the numbers in the notebook. Her memory took her back to her prison cell, after the bell for silence, the time when the prisoners, who were always very tired by then – tired of being cooped up within four walls, tired of thinking, tired of shouting – would simply sit smoking and watching the smoke from their cigarettes unravel, or watching as it was carried off by some draught, some current of air or, perhaps, why not, by a breeze from the sea. Because the sea – the prisoners in the end completely forgot this – was very close to the prison.

"So," Margarita went on, "you've spent forty-seven months in here. If you bear in mind that the average life expectancy of the female population is now seventy-four, that is, eight hundred and eighty-eight months, you have spent 5.35 per cent of your life in prison. Does that seem a lot or a little?"

Margarita liked to play these cruel games, especially during those night-time conversations.

"Which would you prefer? For the lover you had before you came here to go off with another woman, or for him to die in an accident? And another thing, if the devil or your fairy godmother, or both of them together, gave you one wish, just one, what would you ask for? To leave prison or to have a friend of yours who has died come back to life again?"

At first, she had distrusted Margarita and had even thought of asking to change cells because they seemed so ill-matched. What sort of person was she, that woman who talked all the time and revelled in the most morbid thoughts? At the time, the rumour going around the prison – that Margarita had kidnapped a child in order to revenge herself on a man – didn't seem that hard to believe. But after a while, like someone who crosses a frontier and gradually grows used to the climate and the customs of a new country, she began to feel happy in her company. As a cellmate, Margarita was priceless. She was an intelligent, slightly eccentric woman who talked a lot, but who almost always – perhaps because she had worked in the theatre – spoke in different voices, like someone constantly changing roles or like someone who, because of their manic nature, cannot control the ups and downs of their moods.

"So what do you say, does that 5.35 per cent seem a lot to you or a little?"

"Said like that, it doesn't seem very much at all. But it probably is a lot."

"It sounds like a rate of commission," said Antonia, "and since commission is normally about 10 per cent, 5.35 per cent doesn't seem bad at all."

Margarita smiled at Antonia's remark and continued her calculations.

"Of course, it depends how you look at it. For example, if you calculate the time in hours, the commission would come to thirty thousand hours. Imagine the number of films, meals in restaurants, walks in the country or at the beach, all the trips, all the . . . "

"All the hours of work!" Antonia interrupted her. "Out there, I used to work ten hours a day in a canning factory. Those hours don't count. They're no loss. On the contrary."

Antonia had said all this very seriously, but Margarita burst out laughing. She was happy. That day, the game was going well.

"All right, then, I agree to subtract all the dreary hours spent working. So, at ten hours a day, assuming I've got my sums right, your stay in prison will mean a loss of only fifteen thousand hours, good hours, real hours."

"You can take away the hours spent asleep as well. Sleep is the same anywhere. I'm sure there are people living in palaces who sleep worse than I do here."

"You're very inspired today, Antonia. You're absolutely right. Let's subtract those hours too," agreed Margarita. Then she did her calculations. "Eight hours of sleep a day means subtracting twelve thousand hours. Therefore, our beloved colleague here has lost three thousand hours in prison. Only three thousand real hours."

"There's something else too, Margarita. There are the good times that we spend in prison. Good times are good times wherever you are."

"You're right. We're having an excellent time right now. And during these years we've had many moments like this. I think we could lower the number of wasted hours to fifteen hundred."

"I think it should be lower still. You have to bear in mind all the bad times you have outside. Bad times are the same everywhere."

"You're so logical, Antonia. Well, if we err on the low side, in a period of four years you might have about fifteen hundred bad hours. Therefore, if we take away those fifteen hundred hours, the result is zero."

Margarita laughed again, then added:

"Congratulations. You're about to leave prison without ever having been here. It's a shame that mine and Antonia's cases are more serious. It's harder to calculate away our twenty per cent, isn't that right, Antonia?"

"Yes, we're paying way too much commission."

The bus had just reached the top of a long hill from which you could look out on a vast expanse of land. By then, they had left behind them the second city, Barcelona's other side, and now there were mainly vineyards: young vineyards, bright green, separated by lines of cypress trees, with a house here and another further off, far from the motorway. Nevertheless – as she realized when she took a more careful look at what she could see from her window – the victory of the country over the city was still not complete: from time to time, she would see a grimy building, a warehouse perhaps, or a run-down factory, like a tick clinging to the skin.

There was an empty space of about two feet between the roof of the bus and the plastic screen around the driver's seat. The bus was now going down the hill and a strip of blue sky and the red and green lights of a toll station suddenly appeared in that space. Almost simultaneously, as if in sympathy, the video screen filled with coloured stripes.

The bus rumbled across the asphalt surface of the toll station. Shortly afterwards, when the bus continued on its way and drove underneath the archway linking the toll booths, she had the feeling that she was crossing a frontier and that she was finally leaving behind her a part of her life that had lasted exactly three years, ten months and twenty-seven days. Or, rather, twenty-eight days, because she had to include in the accounts the time between leaving prison and starting the journey.

She closed her English notebook and put on the headphones that came in the little red box. The first three channels were broadcasting orchestral music, which was supposed to be relaxing; the fourth was also devoted to music, but interspersed with sports reports; the fifth, connected to the video, reproduced in words the title being shown on the screen at that precise moment. The film they were going to show was called *Eve and the Serpent* and had been passed by the censor.

"The serpent is the most evil of all the creatures in God's creation," she heard a voice intoning through the headphones. On the screen, next to the credits, was a real snake.

The sombre soundtrack wrapped around the words that followed:

"The serpent said unto the woman, Yea, hath God said, Ye shall not eat of every tree of the garden? And the woman said unto the serpent, We may eat of the fruit of the trees of the garden, but of the fruit of the tree which is in the midst of the garden, God hath said, Ye shall not eat of it, neither shall ye touch it, lest ye die."

She took off the headphones and finished drinking her coffee, staring at the backs of the two nuns, whose seats were slightly ahead of hers. If there was any truth in the ironic remark the driver had made before they left Barcelona – he had said that the two nuns would really love the film – they were in for a few rather shocking scenes.

She looked out of the window. The grey covering the sky was becoming thinner and there were more and more patches of blue, especially along the edges, in the distance. In the centre, where the sun was hiding, the grey was taking on yellowish tones as if the sky over there were made of quartz.

The bus was now speeding along the motorway in the best possible direction, towards the bluest part of the horizon. Besides, the purr of the engine had a calming effect, much more so than the orchestral music provided through the headphones, and she thought – suddenly, as if it were a revelation – that she felt well, very well, in harmony with things, contented with what she was hearing and with what she was seeing, with the taste of coffee in her mouth and the smell of her favourite cigarette in the air, as she sat, almost curled up, in that particular corner of the bus, which, for some reason, perhaps because they didn't want to breathe in other people's smoke, no other passenger chose to visit. In fact, as she had noticed already on a couple of occasions, the passengers on the upper deck preferred the hostess to bring them coffee or a drink in their seat. All the better for her; she just hoped it would remain like that for the rest of the trip.

She picked up a book from the pile she had on the table, and looked for a part she had underlined, a quotation from the sculptor Oteiza which she knew almost by heart. It seemed to her that the wellbeing she felt at that moment had a lot to do with what he was describing there, and she wanted to read it again. She needed the books, or rather the people behind the books, to give her a sense of security and to confirm what she was feeling.

> When I was a child in Orio, where I was born, my grand-father used to take us for walks along the beach. I felt terribly drawn to the big hollows scooped out in the part farthest from the sea. I used to lie down and hide in one of them and look up at the great expanse of sky above me, whilst everything else around me disappeared. I felt utterly protected. But what did I need protecting from? As children and ever afterwards, we feel our existence to be nothing, that it is defined for us by a negative circle of things, feelings, limitations, in whose centre, in our own heart, we sense our fear – the supreme denial – of death. My experience as a child lying in that hollow in the sand was that of being in flight from my small nothingness to the great nothingness of the sky into which I would penetrate, in order to escape, in the hope of salvation.

She looked out of the window again. Despite the patches of blue, like holes, like points of entry, her spirit – her nervous spirit, surrounded by negative things – could not penetrate that sky and then stay there floating around like one more cloud. Nevertheless, that vision comforted her, like the monotonous drone of the engine. What speed would the bus be going at? Ninety? As they sped past, she barely had time to study the farms built on the edges of the vineyards.

She put down the book by Oteiza and picked up Stendhal's *Scarlet and Black*. It was a book to which she felt profoundly grateful. The story of Julien Sorel and Madame de Rênal had given her many hours of pleasure at a difficult time, when she had been in prison for about a year, a dull period which began with the death of hope – the sad flower that every prisoner wore pinned in her buttonhole the very day she arrived – and ended in acceptance. Thanks to that book, part of that time, that leaden time, had been rendered weightless.

She opened the book at random and started reading.

> As the sun set, thus hastening the decisive moment, Julien's heart beat unusually fast. Night had fallen. With a joy that removed a great weight from his chest, he realized that it would be a very dark night.

She wanted to continue reading that fragment – another of the bits she had underlined – but she couldn't. The purring of the engine was sweetly lulling her to sleep. Before leaving the book and closing her eyes, she thought that her head no longer ached, that she was feeling better and better, that she was coping really well with the new situation, with the world. That was her last thought. Then she fell asleep and began to dream.

The dream

The dream had several acts, like a play, each with its own characters and its own scenery. Whenever the bus jolted or there was a sudden noise, she would half-open her eyes and almost wake up, and then the scenes would lose some of their purity and re-form with remnants of memory and ideas clinging to the dream the way mud and blades of grass cling to the shoes of someone walking through the forest. Nevertheless, despite these interruptions, the dream, which was fairly long, remained coherent from start to finish.

The scenes in the first part of the dream took place in a large garden, about ten years before, when she was only twenty-seven.

"You see? They'll soon be out," said a rather aristocratic-looking old man, walking on to the stage. With the silver handle of his walking stick he was pointing to a row of cherry trees whose branches were thick with buds.

"It's too early, isn't it? It could still snow," she said. She was standing on a wrought-iron balcony that formed part of the loggia of a beautiful stone house.

"According to something I read the other day, it hasn't snowed in Biarritz in March since 1921," said a third person, taking the stage. He was a young man of delicate appearance, about twenty-three years old, who expressed himself shyly. He was called Larrea, and people said he was there because he was the main representative of the most radical of the political organizations gathered together in the aristocrat's house.

"The main representative of the most radical political organization," she repeated, approaching the frontier between dream and waking, and she suddenly remembered everything surrounding that scene. She and another fifteen militants – all of them members of four different organizations involved in the armed struggle – were meeting in the palace of an aristocrat on the outskirts of Biarritz with the aim of analysing the possibilities of a joint strategy. Three days after the meeting began, they had reached complete agreement except on one point: should they attack all banks, or should they respect those founded originally in the Basque country and with Basque money? On that point, the rather delicate young man and his group had taken one position and everyone else the opposite. The trivial conversation begun by the old aristocrat about the cherry trees had been merely an attempt to relieve the tension arising from that confrontation.

"Shall we go out into the garden?" the aristocrat asked the group gathered in the loggia. "We can sit at the oval table beneath the magnolia tree and have an aperitif. It's more than an hour before supper."

The group gave a murmur of approval.

"You should bring a sweater or a jacket. You'll get cold," Larrea said to her.

The sound of a horn almost woke her from her dream, but a few seconds later, the images of that meeting in Biarritz continued to parade through her mind clearly and precisely, as real as the plastic coffee cup or the books that she had held in her hand. First, she saw the garden belonging to the aristocrat, and in the garden, beneath a magnolia tree, an oval table carved out of stone. Most of the militants who had taken part in the debates were sitting round that table; it was almost dark, because the shade from the tree obscured the little remaining daylight.

Sitting at the table, she had the impression that her mind was thinking of its own accord, and that the ideas it was forming were phenomena as remote from her own will as the chemical reactions taking place in her intestines, as the beating of her heart. Surprisingly – until that moment she had been unaware of what was happening to her – all that involuntary activity revolved around that young man, Larrea. There was only one more day left of the meeting, after which, since both of them belonged to different, almost rival organizations, they would not see each other again.

Knowing this troubled her. Little by little, ignoring the conversation taking place at the table between the aristocrat and her colleagues at the meeting, that initial idea engendered a twin: she could not accept that separation, she had to make contact with Larrea. At once, her mind provided her with a new and strangely attractive possibility: yes, she should make contact with him, but in the literal sense; she must reach out and grasp his hand, right there, before the whole group went upstairs to supper. Luckily, Larrea had sat down near her. They were separated only by the large bulk of a militant known as the Yeti.

The aristocrat had just finished telling an anecdote, and everyone around the table burst out laughing. She did not. She felt more and more troubled. She was beginning to understand; she was beginning to understand what lay behind some of her own attitudes during the debates. She had never once tried to refute the young man's arguments. On the contrary, she had felt uncomfortable when some member of her own group, the Yeti for example, had spoken to him brusquely or disrespect-fully. And during the breaks, during the lunches and suppers too, she had always tried to sit near him.

She sipped at her aperitif and ate the olive that came with the drink. Should she admit it? Should she say that word? It was more than a year since her divorce. Was she in love?

The aristocrat went on talking, trying to take the tension out of the situation. He had a glass in one hand and she could just see the end of the cocktail stick holding the olive above the edge of the glass.

"When he puts the olive in his mouth, I'll take Larrea's hand," she thought. It was not going to be an easy operation, since she had to reach behind the Yeti's back, very carefully, so that no one would notice. What would happen if someone at the table realized? And what if Larrea rejected her hand? Those thoughts made her heart beat faster. It was true that beneath the magnolia tree it was growing ever darker, but the risk – the risk of appearing ridiculous – also seemed to her to be growing ever greater.

She didn't have to wait long for the signal; the aristocrat picked up the cocktail stick and, after various attempts – his eyesight obviously wasn't very good – he managed to place the olive in his mouth. Then he snapped the cocktail stick in two and placed it in one of the ashtrays on the table.

She leaned back and reached her left arm out behind the Yeti's back.

"When are we going to eat? I'm hungry," said someone. Her arm froze.

"Let's finish our drinks first," said the aristocrat.

Between Larrea and the Yeti there was a wider gulf than she had supposed, almost another arm's length. It became even more difficult when the Yeti, misinterpreting her posture – she had leaned her body towards him – drew her to him and started to embrace her, putting an arm around her shoulders.

"It's cold, isn't it?" said one of the other women who was sitting next to the aristocrat, and two or three people agreed. At any moment, people would start to get up from the table.

She freed herself from her colleague's embrace and made a

last attempt to reach Larrea, stretching her arm, her hand, her index finger as far as she could.

Then something ineffable happened. Contrary to all probabilities, the tip of her index finger touched the tip of another index finger. Startled by that unexpected contact, she rapidly withdrew her hand and resumed her normal posture at the table. She looked over at Larrea. He had his arm outstretched too and was holding out his hand to her behind the Yeti's back.

The dream images provoked in her the same shudder she had felt ten years ago in the garden in Biarritz, and she snuggled down in her seat so as to savour that feeling. But she couldn't. The bus, which was still flying along at nearly ninety miles an hour, hit a dip and she nodded a little, enough to interrupt her dream and to force her to open her eyes. For a moment, on the other side of the window, she saw a village surrounded by pine trees and a great strip of blue sky. Nice, she thought, it was nice that blue sky. Then she closed her eyes and tried to go back to the scene in the garden.

It was useless. The dream had taken another direction and a new scene replaced the previous one. She and her colleague in the organization, the one they called the Yeti, were standing in a maritime museum arguing; they were in the room containing the gigantic skeleton of a whale.

"Just what are you up to?" asked the Yeti.

"What do you mean?" she said, walking away towards the whale's tailbone. She felt a stab of pain in her head.

"Do keep still, will you? What I have to tell you is very serious," said the Yeti. He had a clumsy gait and disliked having to move.

Most of the schoolchildren who were visiting the museum at that moment were either looking at the tropical fish aquarium or at the one containing octopuses. Only one little girl had remained apart from the others. She was looking at the black lampreys, at their white teeth. Perhaps she was an image of her? Perhaps she had been like that, a solitary child?

The question provoked by the image in the dream vanished at once. Again she saw the Yeti's face.

"You know perfectly well what I mean. You're going out with that guy Larrea. I know you're seeing each other. I'm certain of it, absolutely certain."

Despite his appearance, he wasn't rough-mannered. He spoke gently, as if it pained him to have to say those words. She sighed and stroked one of the whale's ribs.

"Who told you? The security people?"

"It's very dangerous for the organization, very dangerous indeed."

The Yeti always repeated everything, so that the idea would go in, like a nail into wood.

"Why is it dangerous?"

The words left her mouth without creating any echo inside her at all. Absurd thoughts occurred to her. For example, how big would the whale have been whose skeleton she was looking at?

"The police know about him and all the members of his little group. They tell them what to do."

"That's not true."

What speed could that whale have reached when it lived in the sea? How deep could it dive? Could it go down to where the lampreys lived? The questions came into her mind unbidden.

"I tell you it's true. The police pull the strings and they move. They probably know about you too."

"Look, I know they take a different line on things, but to say that they're under police control is insulting. That's pure sectarianism."

"You can't continue with your relationship. You'll have to

separate immediately. These are not just empty words. It's an order from the organization."

"I'll think about it."

"There's nothing to think about, it's an order, don't you understand, an order!"

The Yeti stopped shouting and gave a long sigh.

"It's an order, an order. You must understand," he said, resuming his sorrowful tone and putting an arm around her shoulder. She burst into tears. The message had at last reached the deepest layer of her consciousness. Yes, now she understood. She would not see Larrea again or, rather, she would see him one more time, just to say goodbye.

She opened her eyes and the light dazzled her. The sun occupied a large part of the sky, the part she could see through the window, and as far as she could make out, it was beating down on a grey desert. How many serpents lived there? What had become of paradise after Eve listened to the serpent? Had it become a grey desert like the one they were crossing? She looked again at what lay outside and she saw a straight line formed by pylons and a flock of crows circling one of them. How many crows lived in that desert?

"I'm asleep," she said to herself in an attempt to exorcize those senseless questions. She snuggled down in her seat again and looked for other images. She wanted the dream to go on.

She spent some moments with her eyes closed, trying to follow the conversations that she could hear in that part of the bus. Then – the voices seemed to grow ever farther off – she saw a flower, a violet-coloured geranium. She knew that she was back inside the dream again. She had seen that flower on her last meeting with Larrea, through the frosted glass of a bathroom window.

"What do you want to do, then, just leave it?" said Larrea. He was having a shower and the hot water was reddening the skin on his arms and shoulders.

"You know I don't," she said from the stool in the bathroom. She was wrapped in a large towel, and was smoking a cigarette.

"I don't think we've got much option," said Larrea, turning off the shower. "I can't ask you to join my organization, and it's the same with you, you can't ask me to join yours. No one would take it seriously. Besides, I really don't think they'd let me in."

The geranium on the other side of the window appeared and disappeared depending on Larrea's movements in the bath.

"The way you put it, we only have two alternatives," she said. "We can either disobey the order and stay together, or we can say goodbye right now."

For the first time since that meeting in the aristocrat's house, there was tension between them.

"We mustn't go thinking we're Romeo and Juliet. We're not a couple of adolescents," said Larrea, picking up a towel and drying himself. He was smiling, but it was as if he were smiling to himself.

"How old were Romeo and Juliet?" she asked him. The decision they were about to take made her voice sound hoarse, huskier than usual.

"I don't know about Romeo, but Juliet was about fifteen or sixteen."

"Then it's true. They were much younger than we are. Anyway, I'm going to get dressed."

She got up from the stool and left the bathroom.

"I suppose you think I don't mind," Larrea said as she was walking down the corridor.

After that, the scene in the dream changed again, and

moved from the bathroom to the Plaza Condorcet, where the house was. She saw Larrea leaving to look for his car while she, standing on the pavement, was wondering what would happen next. Would he leave immediately, without saying goodbye? Ever since that first time, when their hands had met in the darkness, their goodbyes had always followed the same pattern: Larrea would wind down his car window, and, a few yards before he caught up with her, he would stretch out his arm and she would reach out too and their hands would lightly touch.

Larrea drove out of the car park and, keeping to their ritual, he opened his window and put out his arm. For her part, she stepped out on to the road and prepared herself for that gesture of farewell. But for some reason, it didn't work that day. Their two hands didn't touch.

Larrea braked, as if he were going to stop in order to repeat their goodbyes, but in the end he drove on. She didn't know how to react either and simply watched him drive off.

She would never again see her lover. He would die about a fortnight later trying to disembark on a beach in Vizcaya. According to the rumours, the police had set a trap.

Suddenly the Yeti's face appeared on the scene.

"You women just muddle everything up, everything," he shouted. "How can you say that we betrayed him? If we wanted to eliminate him, we could have shot him ourselves! We could have shot him, do you understand? We don't go around giving tip-offs to the police, you know that as well as I do. Look, I'll tell you what, you're obviously very upset. Why don't you go to Paris for a few days until you calm down."

"I don't want to go to Paris. I'd rather be involved in a raid or something."

"You see what you women are like?" The Yeti was tugging at his beard and gesticulating. "No, you're not taking part in any raid. You'll go to Paris. More than that, you'll keep well away from the organization for at least three months."

A new voice entered the scene.

"They're dangerous people all right," it was saying. It was a man's voice. "They spend all those years submitting themselves to a harsh regime of discipline, committing all kinds of atrocities, and then they can't adapt to everyday life. It's just like the soldiers in the Vietnam war."

"The other day, we showed a video about that, about a Vietnam veteran who took some customers in a supermarket hostage for some really stupid reason, because he couldn't find a jar of jam, I think it was."

It was the voice of the hostess on the bus, she was sure of it. Were they talking about her? Her heart began to pound. A few seconds later, the man who was talking to the hostess confirmed her fears.

"Look at her, she's asleep now and she looks like a perfectly normal woman, but she's only been out of prison for a day and already she's been up to mischief. Last night she marked a man for life. She cut him really badly with some sharp object. I don't know quite what the object was, because they're very odd cuts. They're not clean cuts. Anyway, that's why I'm here, to take her back to prison. She's capable of anything, she is."

She seemed to recognize that voice. Wasn't it the man at the station in Barcelona who had offered her a light? That guy with the red tie, was he there? No sooner had she asked herself that question than someone hit her on the knee and she cried out.

She sat up in her seat and opened her eyes. Everything around her was quiet. The hostess was talking to a very big man with a face like a boxer, while, behind her, the two nuns were reading with their faces turned away from the images on the video screen. No, she hadn't really cried out. The cry had remained inside her dream, on the other side, inside that reality which, just then, seemed to her more solid, more intense.

She looked around the bus again, at the tiny space which, despite its apparent immateriality, was now the real stage on which her life was being played out. The nuns continued reading and the hostess was listening to what the passenger who looked like a boxer was saying about the film. The noise of the engine was still there too, gently enfolding everything. In fact, the only things that weren't in their place were her books and her coffee. The books were on the floor and the plastic coffee cup had rolled around the table spilling the dregs.

She gathered the books together, mopped up the coffee with a paper serviette and got to her feet in order to throw it in the bin fixed on the metallic wall of the toilet. For some reason, her movement attracted the attention of the nun with green eyes, who stopped reading and turned towards her. It was only a brief look, but enough to reveal the tension on her face. She was frowning and her face seemed deeply lined.

"Why should you have to watch the film if you don't want to? You should ask them to turn it off," she said, guessing the reason behind that tension.

On the video screen, a maid was running along a gallery in

a palace, pursued by the master of the house, a foppish chap with slicked-down hair. She was wearing a dressing gown with apparently nothing underneath. She would occasionally change direction abruptly, affording the viewer a glimpse of her bottom.

"The hostess says she can't turn it off," replied the nun with green eyes, turning back to her. She was talking loudly, in an energetic voice.

"Why can't she?"

The hostess was aware of the conversation, but didn't want to intervene.

"Apparently that would be depriving the passengers who come downstairs to smoke of seeing the film. Thanks for your concern though. There aren't many people these days who would care about two old nuns like us."

"That's all right," she said, feeling slightly embarrassed. That exchange just confirmed to her the oddness of the situation. That was the first time since she was at school that she had spoken to a nun.

She sat down at the table again and put on the headphones.

"Don't run away, Marie. I bet you'd make a wonderful lover," she heard the man say. On the video screen, the half-naked maid and the fop were face to face in a barn next to the palace.

"What's got into you?" said the maid, taking a step back.

"Come here! I'm master of this house and everything in it," bawled the fop grabbing the maid and tugging at her dressing gown.

"Have you gone mad? You've no right!" protested the maid. She was a very bad actress and pronounced the words flatly.

The film jumped a few frames. The fop appeared in close-up on the screen.

"Forgive me, please!" he whimpered. "I didn't mean to offend you! I love you! Why don't you love me? Please, I beg you, love me in return!"

She put the earphones down on the table and rubbed her eyes with her two hands, as if she wanted to wash them clean. Then she lit a cigarette and sat looking out of the window at the grey desert they were crossing, at the mountains in the distance, at the sky. But she couldn't see anything very clearly, because the sunlight – almost as strong as a summer sun – was piercing the layer of clouds and cloaking everything in a resplendent whiteness.

The bright light inside the bus gave definition to the column of smoke from her cigarette and she amused herself watching its evolutions, following its curls and spirals up to the ceiling where they dissolved into nothing. For a moment, she thought about her life and about the things that she wanted to forget; she thought that she should try to transform part of her life into smoke which, later, like her cigarette smoke, would form spirals and curls that finally vanished into air. Was such alchemy possible? Could life become smoke? Even the worst aspects of life?

Holding her cigarette between her lips, she put two of the books from the table back in her suitcase, the novel by Stendhal and the essay by Oteiza. Then she looked at those remaining in the pile and chose another two books: the anthology of Chinese poetry and the collection of poems by Emily Dickinson.

> Though far apart, the two hearts
> love each other in silence, without speaking.
> The woman sews by the light of the candle,
> the man walks beneath the moon.
> As soon as he reaches the stairs, the man knows
> that his wife is still awake.
> A noise is heard in the silence of the night:
> the noise of scissors falling to the floor.

* * *

Reading that poem took her back to prison. She could see herself lying on the bunk in her cell on a Friday or Saturday night, listening to the laughter of people walking along some street near the prison, listening to that laughter and thinking that, despite everything, love was what mattered most in life. Thinking that the cliché was true, that the Chinese poems were telling the truth, that even the crassest of songs were right about that.

Her eyes drifted back to the window. The hills that had succeeded the grey desert were covered in scrub, apart from a few cultivated areas, but they were still empty. For a moment, she thought about the insects, mice and birds that must live there. Then she thought about the silence that would surround the lives of those beings, and about how hard that life would be. But there was no need to pity them: insects, mice and birds were very strong creatures, prepared to face up to any misfortune.

It was quiet inside the bus too. Nothing was happening, everything was still. The film on the video had ended. The two nuns were dozing in their seats. The hostess was reading a magazine. The passenger who looked like a boxer had gone back to his seat.

"I was quite right," she thought, remembering the letter that she had posted in Barcelona. No, she didn't want to see her friend of recent years again. Fuck off, Andoni. Solitude was preferable to a mediocre relationship. In fact, anything was better than that.

She put out her cigarette and rubbed her face again. She had to put a brake on the impetus driving her thoughts along. She was thinking too much, remembering too much, she was getting too tired.

"I must get a grip on myself," she thought. But she knew

how difficult that was. After four years in prison, surrounded always by the same objects and by the same people, subject to the same timetable day after day, everything that she encountered outside seemed sharp and violent and dragged her spirits off on a kind of roller-coaster ride in which, with dizzying speed, white succeeded black, euphoria succeeded depression, joy succeeded sadness. The worst thing was that these ups and downs wore her out, sapped the energy that she was going to need from tomorrow onwards in the real world, not in the world of her dreams or on that bus travelling along an anonymous, almost abstract motorway. Would she find work? Would they have her back at the hospital where she used to work before? They would not. Or so it seemed from what her father had said in a letter; the new intake of nurses had filled all the posts, the good and the bad.

The bus began to brake and she suddenly found herself looking at the driver of the car that was overtaking them at that moment. He was a slim, well-dressed young man and the back seat of his car was full of newspapers. What did he do? Did he have a permanent job? How much would he earn a month? And how much would nurses earn a month now? The car drove on and the bus turned off to the right. They were approaching a service area. Shortly afterwards, the hostess picked up her microphone and made an announcement to the passengers. The stop would last half an hour.

The bus drove straight past the petrol station and the lorry park, over to the area in front of the motel and the supermarket. There was another bus belonging to the same company parked there, the bus doing the same route in reverse, from Bilbao to Barcelona.

The hostess picked up the microphone again and explained that they would be making the usual change, she and the driver would move over to the other bus, while the hostess and the driver who had come from Bilbao would move into theirs. She wished them a good journey and thanked them on behalf of the company.

"That's good news," she said under her breath, thinking about the promised change, and getting up out of her seat. That was one of the advantages that the bus had over prison. You didn't get stuck with certain people, the unpleasant hostesses were only with you for half the journey.

The passengers on the upper deck started coming down the metal stairs. She picked up her cigarettes and the book by Emily Dickinson and hurried to the door. She wanted to get out as quickly as possible and to be the first at the counter in the cafeteria, so as not to waste a single moment of that half-hour break. She would buy a drink and a sandwich and go and sit on a grassy mound that she had seen as they passed the petrol station. It seemed like a good place from which to study the landscape.

There were lots of cats at the entrance to the motel cafeteria and one of them walked over to her as soon as she got off the bus. It had a black head and back and a white front. It was battered and scarred.

"What makes you think I've got any food? I haven't bought anything yet," she said as she passed it. The cat followed her, its eyes fixed on her hands. "Don't be silly. These aren't edible things. This is a book and this is a cigarette packet," she added. Before she had finished what she was saying, the cat shot off towards a passenger who was getting off the bus carrying a sandwich in his hand.

The counter in the cafeteria was very long and the servers were placed at about three-yard intervals. The two at the end were free and she went over to them.

"I'll have one of those sandwiches and two cans of Heineken," she said.

"What sort of sandwich do you want?" asked one of the servers, lifting the cover on the display cabinet on the counter and picking up a pair of tongs. Almost at the same time, the other took the beers out of the fridge and set them before her. They worked really fast. "There's salad, ham and cheese, cheese, tuna and mayonnaise, anchovy, egg and bacon."

As he named the different sandwiches, he tapped them with the tongs. She found it hard to decide. She was bewildered by such variety.

As they came into the cafeteria, the other passengers formed two lines, one going down to the toilets, the other going over to the counter to order something. A very large woman waved to her from the queue for the toilets.

"Who's that?" she thought, responding to the wave with a nod of her head. The woman's face seemed familiar. Where had she seen her before? In Bilbao, before she was sent to prison?

She hurriedly left the cafeteria and went over to the grassy knoll next to the petrol station. She didn't want to meet anyone from her previous life; even before she had reached Bilbao and her parents' house, she was already dreading the inevitable comments from the neighbours who had known her since she was a child, how are you, don't you worry, you'll soon forget about prison. Even more than their remarks she was dreading the replies she would have to make, smiling, playing dumb, pretending that she didn't know what they were really thinking, poor thing, what's she going to do now, if she wasn't divorced at least she'd have something to fall back on, her father doesn't deserve all this trouble at his age.

"Are you going for a walk?" she heard someone say as she

passed the supermarket next to the cafeteria. This time it was the two nuns who greeted her.

Her mind suddenly lit up. The large woman who had said hello to her in the cafeteria didn't belong to her previous life. She was one of the passengers on the bus, the woman in the next seat in fact, the woman with whom she had exchanged a few words before going down to the smokers' section.

"I'm just going over there. I feel in need of some fresh air," she said to the nuns, pointing to the hillock near the petrol station. The petrol station was red and yellow, and the hillock was covered in bright green grass.

"Enjoy your meal," said the two nuns when they saw the plastic bag she was carrying in her hand.

She had to make a special effort to walk like any ordinary person. She felt an impulse to walk very slowly, or better still, to take sixty-five steps as fast as she could in order simply to turn around and start all over again. That was what she used to do in the women's exercise yard in prison, and after four years of going back and forth thousands of times, that habit had become superimposed on her natural liking for leisurely walks and aimless wanderings. The sixty-five steps had ended up becoming a distance set in stone, a rule.

"Two exercise yards and a half," her feet told her, or so she imagined. She was already at the petrol station. Another exercise yard to go and she would reach the top of the little hill, the observation point she had chosen for the first half hour that she was to spend out in the countryside after four whole years.

A gust of wind whisked a plastic bag from the pile on which it was placed and dragged it across the cement floor. That was the only thing moving. There was no one at the petrol station, at least there didn't seem to be. The gleaming red pumps appeared to have just been placed there, waiting for the first car to arrive. The office door was closed.

The wind carried off two more plastic bags, in the same direction as the first. A moment later, when the noise of the bags brushing against the ground became imperceptible, and silence fell again, the loudspeakers in the roof of the petrol station – she hadn't noticed them until then – began broadcasting the sounds of a choir that mingled human voices with the howls of a dog.

She stopped short. She knew that opening. It belonged to a song that Antonia often used to play on the cassette-player they had in their cell. Yes, the chorus of voices and howling would be followed by an acoustic guitar, and the guitar by the words of a singer talking about a dream he'd had, a lovely dream that turned out to be nothing but a false alarm.

At last, the words she was waiting for emerged from the loudspeaker:

> Last night I dreamt
> that somebody loved me;
> no hope, but no harm,
> just another false alarm.

Was it possible to live without love? Was it bearable to live night after night with no one to put your arms around? What did you do when there were no friends to be found anywhere? The questions arose in her mind one after the other and she clung to them, feeling slightly embarrassed, because that world, the world of songs and sentimental lyrics, was not her world, or at least it hadn't been until she went into prison.

A man in blue overalls came out from behind one of the pumps and forced her to interrupt her thoughts.

"What are you doing standing there?" he shouted. He was carrying an iron bar in one hand.

"Don't get jumpy, I'm not planning a hold-up," she replied, in a firm voice. Then she walked past him and over to the grassy mound.

"Where do you think you're going? That area is the property of the petrol station. We have orders to keep it clean," said the man.

"Oh, fuck off," she replied without turning round.

She put everything she was carrying down on the grass, the book by Emily Dickinson and the bag containing the sandwiches and the beers; then she bent her knees and sat down as she used to during the breaks in the yoga classes that she had attended in prison. Before her, at the far edge of a yellowish plain, there were two trees that must have been extremely tall and strong, but seen from there, seemed as slender as spiders' legs. To the right of those trees, near the horizon, the sky was pale blue; to the left, it was dark blue. The sun was just above the trees, but quite high above the horizon, just where the two blues of the sky joined.

She felt a cool breeze on her face. "Last night I dreamt that somebody loved me," the wind was saying at that moment. "No hope, but no harm, just another false alarm," she added mentally when the wind dropped and fell silent.

She thought about the song again and about the questions that it had suggested to her a moment before. No, you couldn't live without love, just as spiders – the little reddish spiders in prison, for example – could not move through the air without first spinning a thread. Sometimes, because the thread was invisible, it seemed that they could, but that was just an illusion. The thread was necessary, love was necessary. The problem was its fragility. The thread could be broken as easily as, one way or another, could love. If they hadn't killed Larrea . . .

"Don't think about it!" she suddenly exclaimed, thumping

her own head. She had to drive out such ideas. She had to get a grip on herself. After all that time, thinking about Larrea was pointless.

She closed her eyes and began to breathe deeply. The sun touched her right cheek, and at first she tried to concentrate on that feeling of warmth. However, as if her mind couldn't settle there, her thoughts drifted off to the cat that had come to meet her as she got off the bus. What colour was its head? Black? Yes, black. And its back? Did it have a black back too? Yes, it did, she was sure it did. And what about its front? No, its front wasn't black, it was white. And its tail? She couldn't remember anything about its tail, or rather, she remembered that there was a scar right at the base.

She heard a noise, like someone fumbling with a plastic bag, and she opened her eyes. The cat that she had been thinking about was only a yard away from her and was trying to take the sandwiches out of the bag.

"What are you doing here!" she shouted, startled by its sudden appearance. The cat took fright and left the bag alone. "It's like magic!" she said. That unexpected coincidence amused her.

The cat sat down about two yards away, its eyes fixed on the bag.

"Which do you prefer, cheese or salad?" she asked, in a softer tone of voice. She broke off a piece of cheese and put it down on the grass. The cat snapped it up.

"Do you like beer?" she asked it a little later, when the sandwiches were eaten. Ignoring the can of Heineken she offered it, the cat walked over to the other side of the hill and sat gazing at the horizon. The sky was still divided into two different blues, but on the frontier between them, above the tall trees, you could see a line of flat clouds. With a little imagination, you could think of them as flying saucers taking off towards the sun.

She put down the can of beer and opened the book of poems by Emily Dickinson. She wanted to find a favourite of hers, a poem about grass. She had promised herself that the very first opportunity she had to sit down on some grass after leaving prison, she would read the poem out loud.

She found it at once, and started reading it slowly, pronouncing each word like a little girl, or like a sleepwalker. The alcohol in the beer that she had drunk helped her shrug off the embarrassment she still felt whenever she read anything out aloud, even when she was alone.

> The Grass so little has to do –
> A Sphere of simple Green –
> With only Butterflies to brood
> And Bees to entertain –
>
> And stir all day to pretty Tunes
> The Breezes fetch along –
> And hold the Sunshine in its lap
> And bow to everything –
>
> And thread the Dews, all night, like Pearls –
> And make itself so fine
> A Duchess were too common
> For such a noticing –
>
> And even when it dies – to pass
> In Odors so divine –
> Like Lowly spices, lain to sleep –
> Or Spikenards, perishing –
>
> And then, in Sovereign Barns to dwell –
> And dream the Days away,

> The Grass so little has to do
> I wish I were a Hay –

From the loudspeakers in the petrol station came the strains of a march and she walked back to the motel in time to the music. That rest had put her in a good mood.

Instead of going directly back to the bus – there were still five minutes before they had to leave – she went into the supermarket and bought whatever she fancied from the shelves, two Crunchies, a small bottle of moisturiser, a fashion magazine, a magazine about the occult and three newspapers. They were the first things she had bought in a long time, her first real purchases, quite different from buying things at the prison store. She had the feeling that she was gradually changing worlds and becoming integrated into reality again.

"Stop trying to be perfect!" she read on the way out, while she was waiting for the checkout girl to finish dealing with another customer. The words appeared on the cover of a fashion magazine. "Are you obsessively tidy? Are you just about to put all your CDs in alphabetical order? Don't waste your time and energy trying to control this chaotic world of ours. You'll be a happier person for it."

She pulled a face. She hated such fatuous things. No, it wasn't going to be that easy to adapt to reality.

"You've got the right change in your hand," the checkout girl was saying.

"So I have!" sighed the customer ahead of her. It was the large woman who had greeted her in the cafeteria, her travelling companion. "I never used to be this stupid, but ever since my health began to fail, I can't seem to get anything right. Do forgive me."

"Perhaps you need glasses," said the checkout girl.

"No, no, it's not a question of eyesight. It's something much more serious than that. Although, in fact, lately, I've been feeling really well," replied the large woman. Then she turned to her. "What about you? How do you feel after having a cigarette?"

"Pretty good," she said, barely looking up from the magazine. She didn't want to encourage her to go on talking. As soon as she dropped her guard, the woman would regale her with the whole story of her illness in all its details.

"We're alike, you and I," the large woman went on, stopping at the other side of the checkout. "I like to be alone too. I'd much rather be on my own than put up with all the usual disappointments other people seem to suffer."

"I left my seat because I wanted to smoke. It wasn't so that I could be alone," she said, after paying for her purchases.

"I didn't mean that. I meant because I saw you sitting on the grass," said the large woman when they went outside. "Not that I was spying on you. It's just that I had the same idea and I was about to go over when I saw you there. Didn't you have a cat with you too?"

"The cat did follow me, yes."

"For a moment, I thought I'd join you, but you looked so absorbed that I thought it best to leave you alone. You were reading a book, weren't you?"

"Thanks for being so considerate. Not everyone would have been so kind," she said, paying no attention to the last question. "And now, if you'll excuse me, I have to go to the toilet."

"I'll wait for you here. If they don't see anyone waiting outside, they might leave without you."

When she came back, most of the other passengers were already on the bus, but there was still a queue to get on.

"You were quick! You hardly took any time at all. You're obviously very fit," said the large woman.

"I didn't have far to go," she replied, smiling. Then she stood behind the woman and opened the magazine.

"Four ways of increasing your sexual confidence," she read. "First, take risks. Feeling comfortable about some new sexual technique is like diving into the water, says Dr Valle. You have to take a leap. If your fear seems insurmountable, take it one step at a time. That was how a woman having problems with oral sex solved the problem. She started with little kisses and, in the end, she found it all perfectly natural."

"Have you got your ticket?"

The new hostess, a young blonde, was addressing the large woman.

"I suppose so, but I don't know where it is," replied the woman. She seemed flustered.

"Her seat's next to mine. It's number thirty-one," she said to the hostess, showing her ticket.

"OK," said the hostess. She didn't seem as severe as the previous one.

"Thanks very much," said the large woman to the hostess. Then she looked at her. "And thanks for your help. Are you staying downstairs in the smokers' section?"

"There's nothing I love more than a smoke. You know what these vices are like."

The large woman smiled understandingly and disappeared up the stairs.

"Can you bring me a coffee once we set off?" she said to the hostess.

"Of course. Are you staying down here?"

She nodded and sat down in the same place as before. She put the magazine on the table and went on reading.

"You need to be positive about your fantasies, says Dr Valle. In other words, if you dream about Harrison Ford, don't imagine him casting a critical eye over your thighs. Don't feel guilty. We women often fall into that trap. If you get excited thinking about a particular actor, don't imagine you're deceiving your husband. If it makes you feel any better, just remember that he might well be fantasizing about Sharon Stone."

She glanced at her watch and then outside. It was seven in the evening and the sun was nearing the horizon. The spaceship clouds were tinged with gold underneath. The rest of the sky was blue. Pale blue or dark blue.

"Do it over the phone. Sexy phone calls from one office to another can be very exciting. Just make sure the boss isn't listening in!"

"We're off!" said the driver, turning on the engine. He too seemed nicer than the previous one.

The bus crossed the lorry park and headed swiftly for the motorway, impatient to get up speed. Without raising her eyes from the magazine, she took out a cigarette and put it to her lips.

"You smoke too much. Every time I see you you're just getting out another cigarette," said someone beside her. Before she had time to react, a lit match was being held about six inches from her face.

It was the man in the brown suit and the red tie, the same one who had approached her at the railway station in Barcelona. She put the cigarette down on the table and turned towards the window.

"We're making progress. Last time you knocked it out of my hand," said the man, putting the match in the ashtray and sitting down opposite her. He smiled broadly and held out his hand. "My name's Enrique. What's yours?"

She said nothing, watching the red car at that moment overtaking the bus.

The mind of an ex-prisoner
Always returns to prison.
In the street, he passes judges, prosecutors and lawyers,
and the police, though they don't know him,
look at him more than at anyone else,
because his step is not calm or assured,
because his step is far too assured.
Inside him lives
a man condemned for life.

The bus was travelling at about eighty or ninety miles an hour now and heading for the orange lights that flanked the motorway, disappearing off into the horizon. She looked first at those lights and then at the sky. The clouds in the shape of spaceships were becoming tinged with pink and the sun was like a brass coin. The rest was blue, the blue of stained glass, simultaneously dark and brilliant.

"Who buys you those red ties?" she asked the man. He had withdrawn his hand, but he was still smiling.

"I pay for them myself, of course," replied the man calmly. He wasn't looking at her, but at one of the magazines on the table. "'Stephanie of Monaco celebrates her thirtieth birthday'," he read out loud. "How time flies! I didn't think she was that old! But then," his smile grew broader and he looked across at her, "she keeps in good shape. Probably all that weight training she does."

"Wearing a red tie doesn't change anything. You can't disguise the smell," she said. She picked up the Crunchie bar from the table and removed the wrapping.

"What do you mean? That I'm a policeman?" he said, suddenly serious, ignoring the fact that she had addressed him as "tú".

The new hostess on the bus came over to them with a tray.

"Excuse me, was it you who asked for a coffee?"

"Yes it was, thanks," she said. She picked up the cup from the tray and placed it on the table.

"Can you bring me one too? Black, no sugar," said the man, smiling again. He could open or close that smile with the precision of an expert accordionist.

The orange lights flanking the motorway could be seen clearly now. They lit up a large industrial area, and the brightest of the lights marked the tops of factory chimneys. A little further on, the lights of Zaragoza were turning part of the sky red and, from the bus, you could see a single star, the evening star, Venus.

> O Venus, evening star, you bring together everything
> that the magnificent Dawn will scatter;
> you bring the sheep, you bring the goat,
> you bring the shepherd boy back to his mother's side.

The hostess returned with the second cup of coffee. The man thanked her and asked her how much he owed her for the two coffees.

"I don't want you to pay for me," she said, putting her hand in her jacket pocket. "I'll pay for myself," she added, addressing the hostess.

"What shall I do?" said the hostess.

"Let her pay!" shouted one of the passengers who had just come down the stairs, in a tone of voice that was intended to be jocular. It was the passenger who looked like a boxer, the one who had been talking to the other hostess.

"All right," said the man with the red tie, placing his money alongside hers. Then he took a sip of coffee and in a low voice he repeated the question that he had asked a few moments before. "Is that what you think, then, that I'm a policeman?"

"That's exactly what I think," she replied. She took a sip of coffee and then a bite of chocolate.

"What I'm going to say will sound strange to you, but I'm going to say it anyway. I'm here to help you. As a friend."

It seemed as if he were going to go on talking, but instead he stopped. Outside the window, the lights of Zaragoza – the lights of the houses, the lights on the aerials – formed a wall here, a wood there, further off a blotch of yellow. The bus slid along giving her a feeling of weightlessness, as if she were flying.

"You can say what you like, but I'm sure you're a policeman. And you may not be the only one on this bus," she said, glancing at the man who looked like a boxer. She was speaking in a tone of utter indifference, as if her only concern was to avoid getting chocolate on her fingers.

The video screen filled with coloured stripes. The second film of the journey was about to start. Behind the screen, to the right of the driver's compartment, a digital clock said it was twelve minutes past seven. Darkness began to fill the inside of the bus.

"Let me finish, please," said the man in the red tie, holding his cup of coffee with two hands. "I said that I come as a friend, and to prove that, I'm going to tell you the truth. I am a policeman, well, not a policeman exactly, but I work very closely with the police. As you know, the organization of which, until recently, you were a member is at war with the State, and people participate in that war at many different levels. What do you think? Is that a subject that interests you?"

Outside, Zaragoza looked like a city divided in two. One of them was ordinary enough, a mere accumulation of buildings and lights, the other – with its cupolas and towers that seemed etched in Indian ink on the remaining blue of the sky – had an oriental air about it that made her dream fleetingly of a journey to far-off lands. When she was able to, when she could free herself from her persecutors.

The video was just beginning. The screen showed a military parade. The people watching looked like Latin Americans.

"Don't I even merit a response? I've been perfectly frank with you," said the man.

"Finish your coffee and get out of here. If you don't, I will," she replied, screwing up the wrapping from her chocolate bar and stuffing it in the plastic cup.

"Fine. This is just a first contact, and I won't insist. But I'd like to say something, as a friend, as a true friend. Times have changed, Irene, times have changed a lot."

A shiver ran down her spine and she turned brusquely back to the window.

> Goodnight Irene, Irene goodnight,
> Goodnight Irene, Goodnight Irene,
> I'll see you in my dreams.

She knew the song from the tape that Margarita and Antonia had given her for her birthday, and she had the words copied out in one of her notebooks, possibly in several. She liked it, she loved to listen to her own name being sung to her before she went to sleep, and she loved the way the singer said her name, because it removed her from daily reality and transported her to other places, sometimes to Texas or Montana, at others to the streets of her childhood or to unfamiliar regions that she couldn't quite define. But, suddenly, on that bus, her name emerged from the mouth of a policeman.

Margarita was right, she thought. Losers lose everything. She couldn't even protect her name.

"You look sad suddenly," remarked the man with the red tie. "What are you thinking about?"

"About my name," she said. She picked up the cigarette she'd put down on the table and lit it with her lighter.

"It's a very pretty name. I like it. I mean it, Irene."

"I do too normally."

On the screen, three boys were holding up a taxi at gunpoint and one of them, an extremely skinny youth, was forcing the driver to lie down in the back seat of the car. In the following scene, the shots of a military parade shown at the beginning were repeated, this time showing close-ups of the military and civil authorities presiding over it. All of them – the military, the civilians and the boys who had held up the taxi – looked villainous.

"Don't be frightened, Irene. I've already said that I come as a friend. You can trust me. I won't just dump you like your former colleagues."

The man was looking at her over his plastic cup. He had beautiful grey eyes.

"Are you going or not?" she said, putting the books that were still on the table back in her suitcase.

"Don't worry, I'll go as soon as I've finished my coffee," said the man with a sigh. "But, to be frank, Irene, you're behaving like an adolescent. I've been examining your case and I know you've got problems. You find it hard to accept reality, boring everyday reality, and, on the one hand, that's good. For many years I felt the same, I even joined a Maoist group, but after a certain age, you can't go on behaving like that. How can I put it? It's fine being childish when you're a child, even at twenty or twenty-two, being a gullible fool is understandable, but at thirty-four . . . "

"You may have spent a couple of hours studying my file, but you've got a few of your facts wrong. I'm thirty-seven." She paused and put out her cigarette. She didn't feel like smoking.

"Well, you look much younger I must say," said the man in the red tie, opening his smile and immediately closing it again.

"You shouldn't go meddling in other people's lives without their permission," she said with a scornful gesture. "Only a pig would spend his life doing that."

"You're right, we are obliged to do some terrible things in our job," he replied, adopting a melancholy tone. "That's the old argument, isn't it? Does a good end justify the means? I don't honestly know. On the one hand . . . "

"Look, your philosophy of life doesn't interest me in the least," she broke in, putting on her headphones.

On screen, an exhausted-looking man wearing a loose white shirt was saying: "My son wasn't a terrorist. He was a good student. They laid a trap for him, I'm sure of it." He was talking to a very beautiful woman, and on the cane table between them lay a newspaper with a photo of two corpses lying in the gutter. "Two terrorists dead, one seriously injured," said the headline.

She looked away from the screen and looked instead at the fields near the motorway. Here and there, as if born by some miracle out of the parched earth, there were flowering trees in groups of twenty or in lines of five, or two by two, or all alone, in the most unexpected places. Taking the scene as a whole – this was an idea she had after the bus had travelled on for a few miles – what you saw out of the window was like an emigration of trees, an exodus, the long march of trees towards their destiny. They seemed to be travelling west, towards the part of the sky that was still blue. Were they guided by a star? Was Venus guiding them? No, there was no guide. No possibility of flight. The trees could not move.

"I promise you, I'll do everything I can to find out what happened to your son," the woman journalist on the screen was saying to the man in the white shirt. "But, first, I'd like you to take a look at these photos that I found in the newspaper archives. Do you know these men?"

The man looked closely at them.

"I know him very well," he said, pointing at one of the photos. "He's one of my son's friends at university. But I don't know this other man. I've never seen him before. Who is he?"

"Well, he's the only one who survived that so-called shoot-out with the police."

"Your newspaper says that he's seriously injured."

"But I don't believe it myself. The editor is a bit nervous about it all, and he's simply accepted the official version. If he'd analysed . . . "

The journalist's words on the screen were cut off. The man in the red tie had just removed her headphones and was holding them in one hand, whilst with the other – the open palm towards her as if to say "Stop" – he was signalling to her not to get angry.

"I'm sorry, Irene, but you must listen to me. I mean it. We could be friends."

"I don't think so," she said, snatching the headphones from him. The violence of that gesture attracted the attention of the hostess and the passenger who looked like a boxer.

"I can understand your being angry with me, Irene. In other circumstances, I would have behaved more politely and tried not to alarm you. But, please, just give me a few moments, the time it takes to smoke another cigarette. I can't go back to my seat without having told you what I came to tell you. Will you allow me that time? Just until you've smoked one more cigarette."

The man's grey eyes were looking at her hard. She picked up the packet and took out a cigarette.

"All right. That sounds like a reasonable deal – assuming you keep your word," she said, lighting the cigarette.

She felt tired, tired and anxious about something that she could feel like a wound inside her. She wasn't doing very well; the policeman was gaining the upper hand.

"May I take one?" said the man, pointing to the cigarettes. "I've never tried that brand."

No, the policeman didn't need any grand theory about the soul, nor any in-depth analysis of why people act in a certain way. He just needed to know three or four things, obvious things like the fact that a person who has spent four years within the four walls of a prison emerges into the world debilitated and with a great hunger for affection, ready to accept the smallest sign of love, however wretched or obscure. That was exactly what was happening to her: contrary to what her mind was telling her, she was still sitting there listening to the policeman in the red tie or, rather, the policeman with the grey eyes, a man who, she had to admit, did strike her as extremely handsome. In that sense, she was reacting to the signal, and the message – like poison in her guts – was gradually leaching into her soul.

"Look, Irene, I'm going to put things quite bluntly, as a friend, but bluntly," said the man, putting his cigarette down in the ashtray on the table and leaning towards her. His tone of voice was one that called for greater privacy, for more intimate lighting than there was at that moment on the bus. "Your situation looks very bad, Irene. On the one hand, you have no work. On the other, you've become marginalized from the organization by rejecting the party line and asking to leave prison. Lastly, Irene, how can I put it . . . you're still a pretty woman and you still look quite young, but you're getting on a bit. A while ago, you told me you were thirty-seven, and nowadays, well, you know how it is, men prefer young girls, adolescents, and unfortunately, or perhaps fortunately, they get them too; it's really not that hard these days to get an adolescent girl into bed you know."

"Really?" she said, raising her cigarette to her lips.

"No, Irene, it isn't, and that's the fact of the matter. However regrettable it may be, you have to accept it."

She smiled broadly. The man in the red tie's clumsy efforts to convince her had just become painfully obvious. He wasn't the worldly-wise man he seemed. Like a lot of policemen born in remote villages and with an education that almost always began in a seminary, his Catholic upbringing had made a profound impression on his personality. They all had a Virgin Mary in some corner of their heart.

"I have no problem with the facts. It's up to the individual who they have relationships with. That's what your mother did, after all."

For the first time since the conversation had begun, she had found a weak point. The man in the red tie hesitated. He didn't know how to go on.

"It's true," he admitted at last, picking up the cigarette that was burning out on the ashtray on the table. "There is a great deal of sexual freedom nowadays, but . . . "

He left the phrase hanging and moved his face towards hers, at the same time mischievously opening his smile. Did he know about her sexual encounter of the night before? If they had been following her since she left prison, they would.

" . . . but that freedom," the man went on, lowering his voice almost to a whisper, "is only one-way, Irene. You see a lot of older men with young girls of eighteen, but you don't see any women of a certain age with eighteen-year-old boys. That's how things are, Irene."

"That's how you choose to see it."

"Your situation, Irene, does not look good," said the man, taking no notice of her comment. He didn't want to go down that particular road. "One danger you may well have to face is loneliness. You're not going to tell me that, what with problems finding work, problems with relationships, you're not going to end up back in your old haunts, in your old political world . . . You'll find out for yourself, of course, but it doesn't seem like much of a life to me, at least, not what you could call a life. And that's something which, and again, forgive me being so frank, will be of the utmost importance to you after the years you've lost. I think you need new friends and I could be one of them, why not? I can't guarantee I can solve all your problems, but . . . "

She looked away from the grey eyes and up at the video screen. A dog fight was in progress. The journalist, who seemed to be the heroine, was questioning the people at the fight, showing them the photo she had in her hand. Then the camera cut to a very thin young man, with a mean expression on his face, who was watching the woman.

"That's the one who betrayed the other two. He was the traitor of the group and it was all a lie that story about him being wounded," said the man, turning his head to the screen. "I saw the film once in a bar."

"Well, I haven't seen it before. That's why I'd like to see it now," she said, picking up the headphones. She had nearly finished her cigarette.

"On second thoughts, perhaps you should see it. After all, you're a traitor too."

For a moment she couldn't speak.

"And you're a complete and utter shit," she said, leaning back.

"I'm sorry, Irene. I didn't mean to say that," said the man. As if instinctively, he held out his hand to her.

"I've finished my cigarette. Please go."

She stubbed out the cigarette in the ashtray, so hard that the grains from the carbon filter stained her fingers.

"You can wipe your fingers on this," said the man, offering her a paper serviette.

"Aren't you going to keep your promise?"

She felt weak, as if the word – that dirty, wretched word – which, moments before, had come from her companion's mouth, had left her breathless.

"No, I'm not. I can't now. It would be a mistake," said the man fiercely. There was a metallic glint in the depths of his grey eyes. "I don't think you're a traitor. Not at all. It's your former admirers who think that, the many admirers you had before, because an admirer can never allow his idol to change. How many fans would Elvis Presley have now if he was still alive and living the life of a sensible family man? Very few, Irene, very few. Instead, he became a monster and died very young, and so his admirers go in their thousands to visit his grave. And the same thing would happen with you. Because, the fact is, and again forgive my frankness, Irene, your organization is basically a youthful phenomenon, it's not a serious political movement . . . "

"Please, be quiet! You're giving me a headache!" she broke in, clasping her head between her two hands.

"Then I'll explain it to you very briefly. I want us to be friends – both on a personal level and in my capacity as a policeman. All I want is for you to see our point of view. If we don't reach an agreement, fine, nothing more will be said. But, Irene, you must bear in mind . . . "

"Please, leave me alone!"

She clasped her head again. She felt a stab of pain in one temple.

"I'll talk to you quietly, but I won't be silent. Things are looking bad for you, Irene, and I can help you . . . "

He didn't manage to finish his sentence that time either. A shout stopped him:

"For heaven's sake, I can't bear it a moment longer!"

Everyone on the lower deck stared in amazement at the nun with green eyes. She had got up out of her seat and was looking very annoyed.

"What kind of a policeman are you? I can't believe what I've been hearing! Why don't you just leave the young woman in peace! What right have you to pester her?"

She was standing right next to the man with the red tie now, but she was still shouting just as loudly.

"Leave me alone, nobody asked you for your opinion!" said the man. He seemed embarrassed and kept glancing over at the hostess and the passenger who looked like a boxer.

"It's no good pulling faces, sir! And look at me when I'm talking to you!"

"You'll be sorry for this!"

"*You* certainly will!"

"Oh, really," said the man mockingly, but he was clearly intimidated.

The other nun, who was still in her seat, suddenly turned round, her face tense.

"Her brother is a general, a general, do you hear? An important general in the army!" she shrilled in her old lady's voice.

"I really don't give a shit who he is!" said the man, again glancing at the hostess and the passenger who looked like a boxer, but neither of them made a move to intervene.

"You're a fool, you don't know what you're saying," said the nun with green eyes. "But now, be a good Christian and leave this woman in peace. As for you, Irene, and forgive me being so direct, why don't you go back upstairs? You'll be better off up there. This man has no honour. He's a serpent."

"Good advice," Irene said. She got up from her seat and started putting everything that was on the table back into her suitcase. Suddenly, she burst out laughing. The whole situation was a joke. It seemed totally absurd that a person like her should be rescued by two nuns, two members of the Spanish church. Except that, for once, absurdity was on her side.

"You'll be better off upstairs," said the nun with the green eyes as Irene put the last book in her suitcase and left the smokers' section. The man in the red tie was sitting with arms folded, staring hard at some point on the carpet.

"Give my regards to your brother the general," Irene said.

"I will."

She felt light. The sense she had had a few moments before – that the poison was seeping into her soul, that she was losing ground to the policeman – had vanished completely. The nun's intervention had broken the spell, and she could no longer hear the serpent's whispers.

She walked past the hostess and the passenger who looked like a boxer and started going up the stairs, slowly, trying to keep her balance despite the swaying of the bus. She was just about to put her foot on the fifth step when she felt the presence of someone behind her.

"You filthy whore! Just you wait!" said a hoarse voice behind her.

She instinctively jumped onto the next step and reached the upper deck before she had even realized what had happened. It did not take long. It was not the voice of the policeman in the red tie. He wasn't the one who had threatened her. It had been the other one, the passenger who looked like a boxer. She hesitated for a few moments, as if she couldn't quite remember what she had to do, but in the end she started looking for her seat. Was it number thirty-two? She put her hand in her jacket pocket and took out the ticket. Yes, number thirty-two. It was right there, beside the stairs.

The upper deck was in near darkness. It looked like a cinema. Most of the passengers were watching the video.

"I got tired of being downstairs," she said to the large woman by way of greeting. She got no reply. Despite her half-open eyes and the position of her head, erect and looking at one of the screens, she was fast asleep. Irene leaned her suitcase against the seat and sat down carefully so as not to wake her. She felt incapable of talking to anyone.

"Filthy whore!" she heard as soon as she closed her eyes. But this time it was her memory repeating it back to her. Something crumpled inside her, and her head filled with questions, memories, fragments of poems; questions, memories and fragments of poems that were like specks of dust, like foreign bodies floating in the air. Was there no way out? Was there no lasting happiness? Was there no rest? Was there no final link in the chain? After Larrea's death, was everything hopeless? Was the poem right?

> You stood and looked up at the sky and said:
> If I had wings, I too would fly away
> in search of other lands, I too would strike camp
> on a coast planted with yellow banners;
> so that time could better do its work,
> so that I could forget more quickly
> the walls and the people of this city.

"If I had", "I would fly away", "I would strike camp", the hypothetical forms of the verb. The make-up with which language disguises the impossible. No, there was no way out, no hiding place.

She raised her head from the back of the seat and looked out of the window. Out there, the sky was dark blue, almost black; nevertheless, in the spot where the sun had just set there was a slash of green that looked like the sea and in which the clouds formed yellow islands, red harbours, white boats. She remembered the song they used to sing at school after trips to the coast:

> Ixil ixilik dago kaian barrenean
> ontzi txuri polit bat uraren gainean.
> Eta zergatik, zergatik, zergatik
> Zergatik negar egin,
> zeruan izarra dago itsaso aldetik.

> (The pretty white boat is in the harbour.
> The pretty white boat is on the sea.
> I don't . . . I don't want to cry.
> Over the sea there's a star in the sky.)

Above the green sea that she could see from the window there was a star, Venus, the one that collected up everything that had been scattered during the day and returned it home. She would have liked the star to do the same for her, to pick up all the fragments of her life, scattered here and there, and place them in an orderly fashion inside her, like clothes on the shelves of a wardrobe. But no star could do that.

The large woman gave a snort. When she looked at her closely, she realized that she was wearing a wig, slightly askew. It revealed the side of her head, which was completely bald.

As if she had noticed that someone was looking at her, the large woman changed position.

"Filthy whore!" she heard again. She wanted to forget about the incident on the stairs, but she couldn't.

There were some headphones on the large woman's lap. She

picked them up and put them on. The screen that corresponded to her area of the bus was quite close, and she could see it easily.

"Why do you get into these messes?" the newspaper editor was saying to the beautiful journalist involved in investigating the deaths of the students. The editor was wearing braces and was sweating heavily. The woman was wearing a very elegant white dress.

"And what about you? Why do *you* get yourself into these messes?" replied the journalist in an aggressive tone.

"I don't know what you mean, Miriam."

"It's so obvious, Jack. You've done everything you can to put me off the track, and that can only mean that you're implicated too."

"What do you mean, Miriam? You know perfectly well what my position on the matter is. I've always fought for a decent democracy in Puerto Rico! I'm still fighting for it."

"Really? How exactly? By setting a deadly trap for two students?"

"Miriam, please! Think what you're saying!"

The beautiful journalist opened her handbag and took out a photograph.

"Look at this, Jack," she said to the editor, showing it to him. "They make an odd assortment, don't you think? The one on the left is Cisneros, the most anti-nationalist politician in Puerto Rico. And the other one, in the second row, is Taylor, the FBI man who was sent here by Washington last year."

"Come on, Miriam, don't be so suspicious. They probably just happened to coincide at the same official dinner."

"Exactly, Jack. It was an official dinner. The one that our newspaper organized a month ago."

"That's got nothing to do with it."

"I think it has. Look who's wearing a waiter's uniform. Don't you recognize him? Don't you recognize that skinny boy? He's a bit far from the camera, but even so there's no mistaking him."

"Who is he? I don't know him."

"He's the third man, Jack, the third member of the group who supposedly tried to break up the military parade. He's the traitor, Jack, the one who betrayed the other two."

"He wasn't a traitor, he was an infiltrator working with the police," Irene said, removing the headphones and almost addressing the screen out loud. Then she closed her eyes and sighed. How many more times would she have to stumble over that word? How many more times would someone speak to her of betrayal before the day was over? Yes, Margarita was right. According to her, problems, especially if they were serious ones, acted like malignant magnets that attracted all kinds of painful particles:

"Say some man has left you. You turn on the radio and all the songs are about lost loves and how sad it is to lose a lover. Say you've got to have an operation. You open a newspaper and the first thing you see is an article all about the dangers of anaesthetics. Basically, life stinks."

She didn't feel inferior to anyone, on the contrary. She saw herself – she had said as much to Antonia and Margarita during some of their talks – as a person who had taken decisions, nine or ten important decisions in the space of about twenty years, and that record, regardless of whether the decisions were right or wrong, was, in her opinion, an achievement, because it was the opposite of what mediocrities do, people who just let themselves drift, never deciding anything, just going where the current takes them, whichever current happens along. Nevertheless, words like "betrayal" intimidated her and made her doubt herself. Not because there was necessarily any truth in them – in that respect, her conscience was clear – but because they were essentially grubby words, words that always left a stain, even when they emerged a penny a dozen from the lips of a complete and utter bastard or were written by the hand of a fool. The policeman with the red tie had called her a "traitor". Many others would do the same. On the walls of Bilbao, some adolescent would doubtless put the accusation in writing.

She remembered a letter that she had read months before in the newspaper. In it, a militant who had opted for the same path she was taking pleaded for respect and published his own past record for the benefit of those who despised what he had done, his so-called "repentance", setting out everything that he had gone through in his fight for an ideal. A letter written in vain? She thought so. As individuals, people weren't bad, but in a group, in the safety of anonymity, people became monsters. Could you expect compassion from a monster? Only in stories – fairy stories.

She sighed again. She didn't want to dwell on the subject any longer, not until more time had passed. Besides, she had quite enough to deal with on the bus, with the two policemen. Would they approach her again? Would they just give up for the present? She mustn't think about it. It was best to pass the time watching the film.

On the screen, the infiltrator who had pushed the two university students to their deaths was smiling at the journalist.

"You're very beautiful. I'd like to be your friend. I'm nicer than I seem," he said.

"I want to know exactly who you're working for," replied the journalist very gravely.

Suddenly, she remembered that there were other channels, apart from the one connected to the video, and she twiddled the knob on the arm of her seat. The dialogue between the infiltrator and the journalist broke off and was replaced by flute music. It wasn't any ordinary flute, it had the deep tones of a harmonium. The musician – she imagined him as a shepherd playing in some new Arcadia – lengthened out each note and the melody came and went, as if forming waves, ever slower, ever deeper.

She looked at the large woman. She was still in the same position, her head erect and her mouth half-open.

"I wonder if she's dead," she thought. Just at that moment, the woman muttered something and shifted in her seat.

She felt tired again. The tension of her encounter with the two policemen had drained her of energy. Or was it the flute? She had the sense that the sound reaching her through the headphones was gradually emptying her of feelings.

She looked out of the window. Outside, everything was in darkness, and all she could see were the lights of the cars coming in the opposite direction and what they illuminated. She screwed up her eyes to see better, but she still couldn't really see anything clearly. And Venus? Was it still in the sky? She wanted to look up, but she couldn't. Her eyelids were growing heavy. Shortly afterwards, she fell asleep and began to dream.

Second dream

As soon as she fell asleep, a feeling of strangeness came over her. She saw herself beneath a completely blue sky and in an unknown place that was nothing like the bus. And it wasn't only what she saw that was strange, there were strange noises and smells too: the birdsong, the tinkling cowbells, the fragrance of rosemary and thyme.

"What is this place?" she thought, and the effort of trying to find an answer almost woke her up. But what she could see, smell and hear was so pleasant that she decided, right at the last moment, just as she was about to open her eyes, to go on and to immerse herself in that new reality.

She examined what there was beneath that blue sky. She saw sheep, lambs and a hut.

"Of course, that's why I could hear bells," she thought. Then she reached out her hand towards one of the lambs nearby and gathered it into her lap. It had a black head and its tail was light brown, but the rest of its body was completely white. It smelled really good.

Suddenly she noticed Margarita. She was sitting at the door of the hut and had a book in her hands. Next to her, lying on the grass, was a huge dog, a greyhound.

"I'm going to read you a poem, Irene. I think it fits your new situation perfectly. You look just like a shepherdess," Margarita said, opening the book.

How could that be? Had Margarita left prison too? In that case, where were they? In Argentina? On the Pampas? She raised her head and looked around. All about her was a vast meadow. Yes, they could well be in the middle of the Pampas.

She had to interrupt her thoughts. Margarita was beginning to read.

> Little Lamb, who made thee?
> Dost thou know who made thee?
> Gave thee life, and bid thee feed
> By the stream and o'er the mead;
> Gave thee clothing of delight,
> Softest clothing, woolly, bright;
> Gave thee such a tender voice,
> Making all the vales rejoice?
> Little Lamb, who made thee?
> Dost thou know who made thee?

She started stroking the lamb. She felt a great feeling of calm, or something beyond calm; quietness, stillness, trust, serenity. Occasionally, a gust of wind brushed her hair, but it did not feel in the least cold. Was that what the Pampas were like? A kind of Arcadia? Perhaps it was. There was the flock, there was the blue sky, there too, although she had not heard it until then, was the sweet sound of the flute. Where was the shepherd flautist? She looked everywhere for him; she scanned the banks of a lake near the hut, she peered into the shadows of the willows bent over the water, but she could see no one.

The sheep had begun to move towards the lake, closely followed by their lambs. The sun was high and the water glittered.

"Do you want to go too?" she asked the lamb in her lap. The animal did not move.

"You were quite right to come here," said Margarita, standing in the door of the hut. She too seemed calmer than when they had been in prison. "Life is very simple in this part of the world. You can get by on very little here. Do you know why? Because there are no people."

"No people?"

"Very few. There are no more than two hundred inhabitants in the whole region. It's a twenty-minute ride to our nearest neighbour. Life is very easy in conditions like this."

"The green desert," she remarked, gazing into the distance.

"This is your place, Irene," said Margarita. She got up from the door of the hut, walked over to where Irene was sitting and lay down on the grass. "The way things were, you couldn't return to your own country. Why struggle to rebuild your life in the places of the past? It seems fine to me that Antonia should do it, or the prostitutes and gypsies who were with us, because they all had somewhere to go, they had someone waiting for them. But you? What awaited you in Bilbao? I'll tell you, Irene. First, a cement wall with the words "informer" and "traitor" scrawled on it; second, the baleful looks and the hatred of your former friends; third, the pity of people of good conscience; fourth, insidious persecution by the police, trying in a thousand and one different ways to get information out of you; fifth, the indifference of that family of yours who scarcely ever visited you while you were in prison. In a word, Irene, hell. That is all you would have found in the places of the past."

"You're right," she said. "Besides, my previous world doesn't interest me at all. I mean, there are some situations, however awful, which can still seem attractive, but not in this case. During my last year in prison, I couldn't bear to read the newspapers or the bulletins they sent me from the Basque country. They bored me."

"I'm not surprised, Irene. That was something I could never understand, how a restless person like you could still belong to the stagnant world of your former colleagues."

The lamb jumped out of her lap and ran over to the lake.

The greyhound that had been lying at the door of the hut came over and lay down beside Margarita. It was the same colour as the lamb: white, brown and black.

"It's called Run Run," said Margarita. The dog wagged its tail.

"Why Run Run?" she asked. This time the dog looked up.

"Don't you know the song?"

She shook her head.

"Shall I sing it for you?"

"All right."

"I used to sing it every day, not just once, but often. But now, I'm not sure, I may not remember it all."

While Margarita concentrated, she stroked the dog's head and back. The moment seemed utterly delicious. It was the same as when they used to get together in the sanctum sanctorum in prison, only this time with the dog, the lambs, the blue sky and everything else. She folded her arms and waited for the song. Someone she couldn't see started playing the guitar to accompany Margarita.

> Aboard a train of oblivion,
> before the break of day,
> at a railway halt in time,
> all ready and eager to go,
> Run Run headed north,
> don't know when he'll be back.
> I'll be back for the anniversary
> of our solitude, he said.
>
> Three days later a letter
> written in bright red ink
> told me that his journey
> might last longer than he thought,
> that this, that and the other,

that he never, and besides,
that life is all a lie
and only death is real,
ay, ay, ay de mí.

Run Run sent the letter
just for the hell of it.
Run Run headed north
while I stayed in the south,
between us lies a gulf,
no music and no light,
ay, ay, ay de mí.

"It goes on, but I can't remember the rest of it," said Margarita, patting the greyhound's head.

"Why do you like that song?" she asked, rather mischievously, remembering what people used to say in prison, that Margarita had been disappointed in love and that in this lay the root of her problems with the law.

"It helps me to get things off my chest. As you know, something similar happened to me. But his name wasn't Run Run and he didn't go north. He went to Spain, to direct a play in Barcelona."

"What was his name?"

"He was the director of the theatre company I was working in. His name doesn't matter. It's an old, old story now. Not like yours."

"Mine?"

"Yours, yes. Your affair with Larrea."

"Larrea was killed," she said, looking away. A group of parrots were fluttering around near the lake. They were green, red and yellow. The flock of sheep had disappeared from view.

"Hold out your hand," said Margarita, almost laughing. "Hold out your hand like God and Adam in the painting by Michelangelo, and see what happens."

She closed her eyes to concentrate better. What did Margarita mean? That Larrea was there too? That he hadn't been killed? That he had managed to flee to the Pampas?

"If only it were true," she sighed. It seemed to her a marvellous place to be, far from her former world, with Margarita, with Larrea. A poem she had read somewhere declared that collecting milk in wooden bowls, tending cows, mending old shoes, making bread and wine, sowing garlic and collecting warm eggs were the only truly important tasks. If there was any truth in that, and if she could count on a little love and friendship from a few people, a new life was still possible.

"Hold out your hand! Hold it out!" Margarita insisted.

She did as her friend asked and she groped for Larrea's hand, just as she had on that first night, just as they had every time they had said goodbye on the outskirts of Biarritz.

She didn't find the hand. Someone grabbed her wrist and forced her awake. The dream had ended.

"You nearly put my eye out with your finger," said the large woman, adjusting her wig. "But that wasn't why I woke you up. I need to go to the toilet."

The red numbers on the digital clock showed ten past nine, and the blackness of night covered all the windows in the bus. Inside, now that the video was over, only the bluish lights in the ceiling were still lit, on guard. The engine sang a single note and produced a kind of buzzing curtain of sound isolating that metallic enclosure from the rest of the world. They were still speeding towards Bilbao.

"I'm sorry. I didn't think it was so late," she said to the large woman. She hadn't quite woken up.

"We'll be in Bilbao in less than an hour," said the woman, without moving from her seat.

Irene realized that the headphones were on the floor. She found it hard to keep her eyes open. "I seem to drop everything," she said, bending down. Her jacket was on the floor too.

"The same thing happens to me," said the woman. "Before, though, I never used to drop anything."

Irene recalled a fragment from her dream and smiled faintly. Just before Margarita started singing, the lamb on her lap had run over towards the lake. That fragment obviously corresponded to the moment when her jacket had fallen off her lap. It was amazing how dreams could transform things.

After retrieving her jacket, she picked up the headphones and held them to one ear. They were playing Latin American songs similar to "Run Run".

"I noticed that on you before," said the large woman, pointing to her jacket.

"What did you notice before?" she asked, placing the headphones on the arm of her seat. She was more awake now.

"The red AIDS ribbon."

"Yes, I always wear it."

That wasn't quite true. In prison, they weren't allowed to wear the ribbon because of the safety pin. Nevertheless, her answer expressed what she would have wished to do. In the four years that she had been in prison, she had seen sixteen young girls die, and she had decided to wear that symbol until the day someone found a cure for the illness. Would modern equivalents of Fleming, Chain and Florey emerge? She had read a book about the discovery of penicillin and greatly admired these three biologists. She had felt very insignificant in comparison.

"You don't know how happy that makes me," said the large woman, placing a hand on her arm. "I didn't say anything before, but I've been gravely ill myself. Really."

"I believe you. You mentioned something about it earlier."

She didn't much feel like talking, but she owed that woman a conversation, she had a bond with her. After all, did not those marked by sickness and by prison belong to the same province? Both carried a mark that set them apart from the other people on the bus.

"Yes, I've been close to death a couple of times and do you know something? There's no reason to fear death. Death is sweet. If you die and the doctors bring you back to life, you feel really angry. You don't want to come back."

"I don't know if I can agree with you there," she said, taking out her packet of cigarettes. She felt like smoking. "That happens with certain dreams, where you'd like to stay inside them for ever, but with death, I'm not sure."

"It's just the same, really it is!" exclaimed the woman, somewhat agitated. "What's wrong? Do you want to smoke?" she asked, pointing to the cigarettes. "Why don't we both go downstairs? As I said, I need to go to the toilet."

"I'd rather stay here right now, actually. The engine's so noisy downstairs."

The large woman made a face, as if she couldn't believe what she had just heard. But she said nothing.

"Go to the toilet. We'll talk afterwards," she said, to calm the woman. Then she got out of her seat and stood in the aisle to help the woman up.

"I haven't upset you, have I?"

"Not at all. When you come back, we'll carry on talking."

The bus started to brake and, shortly afterwards, at the end of a long bend, the green and red lights of the toll booths came into view. Where were they exactly? She looked to either side of the bus and saw three fairly large towns, with populations of maybe twenty thousand each. Could one of them be Tarazona? When her mother had been alive, they had gone there together, to Tarazona – to the Hotel Uriz, the first hotel she had ever stayed in – and to the monastery of Veruela, where the poet Bécquer had spent a long period of time. Like all the teachers of her age, her mother had been mad about Bécquer's poems, poems that she would recite to her at the drop of a hat. What were those poems like? "The dark swallows will return to their nests beneath your balcony, but those who were witness to our love, they will never return," one of them said, more or less. Yes, she had had a happy childhood, but memories were not much use to her. Like dreams, they only managed to salvage the occasional isolated moment. The rest of the time, in everyday life, the present dominated.

The area around the toll booths was very brightly lit, and many of the sleeping passengers stirred in their seats. A blue panel indicated that it was only another forty miles to Bilbao. So that large town near the motorway couldn't possibly be Tarazona. So . . .

She interrupted the thread of her thoughts and, for the first time since she began the journey, she thought about Bilbao, searching out the images hidden behind that name. And from amongst them all, she chose that of the rooftops in the old part of the city, the roofs that she had always seen from her house; hundreds of rooftops, matt red in colour, with the rain falling on them. She felt nostalgic for that rain. How long had it been since she felt the soft rain of Bilbao on her face? It wasn't just four years. She had had to leave the city a long time before she went to prison.

When they left the toll booths for the darkness of the motorway, the glass in the windows became polished surfaces, mirrors. However hard she tried, she couldn't see what was happening in the sky – if there was a moon, if there were stars. In the window she could see only her own reflection, her short hair, small ears, puffy eyes. "So here we are, Irene," she thought, addressing her own image.

The policeman who looked like a boxer attacked her precisely at that moment. She noticed a strange movement behind her, as if two arms were trying to embrace her, and immediately, before she had time to realize what was happening, she was impelled into the other seat and hurled against the window. She felt a sharp pain in her side, she couldn't breathe. She, nonetheless, tried to cry out.

"Shut up, you whore!" said the policeman, putting his hand over her mouth. He was speaking to her in a whisper, so that not even the passengers closest to them could hear him. All she could see was his flattened nose and his puffy eyes, puffier even than her own. "If you scream, I swear I'll break something," he added, again thrusting his fist into her side.

The pain brought tears to her eyes. She couldn't breathe. She couldn't open her mouth to shout.

"I don't want any complications, but if I have to hit you, I will. I'll beat you up and break a couple of your ribs. Do you understand?" said the policeman, panting. He was very strong, but he was much too fat. "Do you understand or not?" he repeated.

She nodded.

"Fine, that's how I like it," he whispered, removing his hand from her mouth. "Don't go thinking that I'm like that handsome colleague of mine. He's soft, especially with girls. I'm not like that, believe me."

He smiled. Beneath the flattened nose was a small moustache beaded with sweat.

"What do you want from me? A magic formula for losing weight?" she said, after taking a deep breath. She saw that her jacket had fallen on the floor again and she bent down to pick it up.

"Be very careful what you do," said the policeman, watching her every move. "And talk quietly, if you don't mind."

"I want to smoke a cigarette. As you know, it helps in tense situations."

She still couldn't breathe normally. She was a bit frightened.

"You can't smoke up here."

She thought of some cutting remark, but decided to adopt a different tone. In her situation, a cigarette could prove very helpful.

"Just the one," she said.

The policeman smiled again. He took something out of the

inside pocket of his jacket. A square bit of paper.

"What do you want to do? This?" he said, pressing a button on the ceiling that switched on a small light.

The square bit of paper was a Polaroid photograph. It showed a man's naked trunk, criss-crossed with bloody lines.

"You certainly left your mark on him," said the policeman.

"I don't know what you're talking about," she said, lighting a cigarette and inhaling the smoke. She had to be careful. She had very little room for manoeuvre.

"Oh yes you do," said the policeman with a sigh. He put the photograph away.

"What do you want?" she asked, exhaling the smoke hard.

"We need your collaboration. We want you to collaborate with us."

"Well, at least you don't beat about the bush."

"I don't like wasting time. I don't like it at all. I leave that to the handsome policemen."

He was very fat around the eyes, which were dull, unhealthy-looking. She wondered what his attitude to sex would be? Probably not exactly wholesome. What would he be like with women? Would he beat them?

"Let me make myself even clearer," the policeman went on. The noise of the bus engine had grown louder and he had to raise his voice. "We have some very concrete proposals to make to you. If you want to collaborate with us, everything will be fine. We'll give you protection, new papers, a house, a good salary . . . "

"Until when? For the rest of my life? How much information do you think I have?" she said, almost laughing. She took another drag on her cigarette and managed to blow the smoke far enough to bother the passengers in front of them. One of them fanned the air with a magazine.

"Until when? Well, we'll have to see. To start with, we have a special task for you. We want to find out about how Larrea died. We think the time has come to find out what really happened."

"Why don't you look to your own house first? You killed him, didn't you?" she said in the most neutral of voices. But the news had startled her.

"That's one possibility, but we'd like to examine all the possibilities, not just one. We'd like to go over the meeting you had about five years ago in the palace of a certain aristocrat. How's your memory for faces? If we showed you some photographs, could you recognize the people who were there?"

"I have no idea what you're talking about, really I don't," she said, blowing more cigarette smoke in the direction of the passengers in front. It was her only way out. She had to get them annoyed, so that they would interrupt that interrogation. It was clear that the large woman was being detained downstairs and was unable to come back up.

The policeman snorted. His flattened nose meant that he couldn't breathe properly.

"You do, but you don't want to tell me. That seems perfectly normal. You haven't heard the rest of my proposal. And that's exactly what I want to do now, lay the whole proposal out to you."

The two passengers in front – a couple – were muttering about the smoke, but still didn't have the courage to protest. If they didn't react, she would stay there corralled by the policeman for as long as he wanted.

"Get to the point. I don't like wasting time either," she said.

"Don't worry, it won't take long. I just have to put the downside of the proposal to you – what would happen if you don't collaborate with us," replied the policeman. He seemed quite calm. He was smiling. "Can't you guess? Can't you guess what would happen to you?"

"I've no idea."

She put her cigarette to her lips. She was annoyed with the couple in front. They seemed prepared to put up with as much smoke as she could blow at them.

"Well, we'll just circulate the photograph. That should be enough," said the policeman.

"Enough?" she laughed. "To start with, you've no proof. And even if you had, I don't care. I'll say it was self-defence, that he was trying to rape me."

The policeman laughed.

"Besides, if the worst came to the worst, I wouldn't get a very long sentence. To judge by the photo, he only had a few cuts."

The policeman looked at her mockingly.

"I wasn't referring to that photo. I meant this one."

It was another Polaroid. It showed her and the policeman with the red tie sitting in the smokers' section downstairs. She was eating a Crunchie bar and he was smiling and talking.

"Take a good look at it," said the policeman, offering her the photograph. "And if you want to tear it up, do so. That one didn't come out very well, it's too dark. The others turned out much better."

It showed a couple talking animatedly. It was taken from the service area, from the bottom of the stairs. When exactly? In the scrap of sky that appeared in one corner of the photo you could see some orange-coloured clouds and a yellowish circle, the last sun of the day.

"There wasn't much light," explained the policeman, guessing her thoughts. "But I have a very special camera, very quiet and very sensitive."

"And what are you going to do with this?" she said at last.

Her cigarette was coming to an end. Not counting the filter, she had little more than half an inch left. And the couple in front were still only muttering and occasionally waving away the smoke with a magazine, but still they did not raise their voices. What more could she do? She had to put an end to that siege. What if she started shouting? Perhaps that was a way out, but she was frightened of the policeman's strength. Her ribs still hurt.

"As I've already said, if you don't want to collaborate with us, we'll put those photos into circulation. And then you'll see. Before the month is out, some journalist will write an article about your life: 'The price of freedom. The pacts terrorists make in order to get out of prison,' or something like that."

The policeman was looking up at the ceiling, as if the headline of the article were written there.

"We'll issue a statement denying it all," he went on, "but, of course, my colleague is too handsome to go unnoticed. Many of your former friends know him. They've seen him at the police station, I mean. I believe they call him Valentino. Anyway, I don't want to hold you up any longer. I think I've made myself clear. Five or six articles about repentant terrorists who've betrayed the sacred cause and then bang, it's all over."

"Fine, I'll consider your proposal. Now, please, leave me alone."

"No way. I've no intention of leaving you alone. I'm going with you as far as Bilbao. I want a reply before we get there. If it's 'yes', you'll come with us. If it's 'no', ... "

The policeman snorted and turned towards her.

"If it's 'no', dear Irene," he went on, stressing every syllable, "if it's 'no' . . . "

"I know. The photos will appear in the newspapers, and bang," she broke in.

"But before that, there'll be the odd broken bone. You've no idea how I long to do it, Irene. I'd almost prefer it if you said 'no'. I'm only doing this because I have no option but to obey orders, but if it was up to me I'd finish off the lot of you once and for all."

Again she felt the policeman's fist in her ribs and couldn't suppress a cry. For a second, she imagined a passenger coming over to them and asking them what was going on, but she immediately dismissed the possibility. The bus was still speeding along, its engine humming, people had their eyes closed and were dozing. She felt like giving up, like dying. She should have foreseen what was going to happen to her. She knew poems that spoke of it, poems that told the truth.

> The Whole of it came not at once –
> 'Twas Murder by degrees –
> A Thrust – and then for Life a chance –
> The Bliss to cauterize –
>
> The Cat reprieves the Mouse
> She eases from her teeth
> Just long enough for Hope to tease –
> Then mashes it to death –
>
> 'Tis Life's award – to die –
> Contenteder if once –
> Than dying half – then rallying
> For consciouser Eclipse –

Suddenly it was as if her head and her hand began to operate independently. While her head was filling with dark thoughts, her hand grasped the cigarette. It was almost finished, but there was still a glowing tip above the filter. She reached her arm over the seat in front and let it drop onto the skirt of the woman sitting there. She heard a shriek.

"Who did that? Who did that?" asked the young man travelling with the woman, stepping out into the aisle and looking at the policeman. He was so upset he could barely speak, he just kept repeating the question over and over, "Who did that? Who did that?" The policeman withdrew his fist from her side.

The aisle began to fill with passengers. No, it wasn't right. No one respects the no smoking rules. What a cheek, smoking upstairs when there was a special section set aside for smokers downstairs.

The policeman didn't react.

"What happened?" asked someone from behind. No one answered. They were all looking at the policeman, albeit rather warily. His burly appearance inspired respect. Someone switched on the main light. It seemed as if no one was in their own seat.

"Why did you do that, eh? Why did you do it?" said the young man, addressing the policeman. He felt humiliated.

"It was the girl. It was the girl who was smoking," said a little boy, pointing at her.

"Really? Is that true?" asked the young man, rather disconcerted. He seemed like a decent chap.

"Yes, it's true. I saw her," said the little boy.

"Why did you do that? My wife is pregnant," said the young man. After that first reaction, he didn't know what to do.

"And what if I wasn't pregnant? Would it have been all right if she'd done it then?" said the young man's wife from her seat. "It doesn't matter, Eduardo. There's no point talking to crazy people like her."

There was a silence. Almost all the passengers had returned to their seats. The incident was about to end as quickly as it had begun. Very soon the hum of the bus would again occupy the foreground and the journey would continue as before.

"Did I burn you?" she asked, standing up and addressing the woman in the seat in front.

"No, but you nearly made a hole in my dress," said the woman sharply.

"I'd like to compensate you in some way," she said. She put on her jacket in one movement and reached out her arm towards the young man, who was still in the aisle. "Can you help me? My companion here takes up such a lot of room and he won't let me out."

The policeman was moving his chin and mouth as if trying to suck in the ends of his moustache. Would he stop her getting out? After the incident, it wasn't very likely. The passengers might make even more fuss, and one of them might easily denounce him to the press. In that case, the newspaper article wouldn't be the one he had predicted – "The price of freedom. The pacts terrorists make to get out of prison" – but something very different, accusing the police of blackmail. Besides, the policeman seemed at a loss to know what to do in a situation like that.

Nothing happened. The young man took her hand and pulled hard, while she rested her other hand on the back of the seat and jumped into the aisle. Once free, she opened the suitcase and took out the picture of Adam and God reaching out to each other.

"It's lovely!" said the young man. The two passengers occupying the seats on the other side of the aisle nodded approvingly. They liked it too.

"It's a copy," she said. "I'd like you to have it."

"It's lovely!" said the young man again, taking the picture and holding it so that his wife could see. "Who is it by?"

"It's on the ceiling of the Sistine Chapel."

"We spent our honeymoon in Italy, but we didn't go to any museums," said the young man.

"This copy was made by a woman in prison. Her name's Margarita."

"It doesn't matter. It's still lovely."

She was about to say that it was lovely precisely because of that, because it had been made in prison, because the maker of the copy had had an awful lot of time to work on it, but she decided not to. At last, she was in the aisle, safe. She picked up her suitcase and went downstairs.

The bus was heading down to the bottom of a valley above which you could see the coppery glow of the lights of Bilbao. The journey would soon be over. Less than half an hour. What could she do until then? How could she keep the two policemen at bay? She only knew three people on the bus, the two nuns and the large woman. Only they could protect her.

The three of them – the large woman and the two nuns – were sitting in the downstairs compartment. Beside the coffee machine, leaning on the small counter, the policeman in the red tie was chatting to the hostess.

"Would you bring me a cup of coffee, please?" she said to the hostess as she passed. As soon as he saw her, the policeman in the red tie gave an alarmed glance up the stairs. He couldn't understand what had happened. Where was his colleague?

"Ah, there you are, at last," said the nun with green eyes by way of greeting. She sounded worried. "What did they do to you? That man told us that they had to interrogate you, that they had some grave matter to sort out with you."

"That's what they said, and they wouldn't let me go back upstairs," added the large lady, casting a glance at the policeman.

"And what grave matter was that?" she asked, taking off

her jacket. She felt suddenly hot.

"A bomb," said the other nun. Close to, she seemed even older. She was angry.

"They don't have much imagination," she said, as she took out a cigarette and lit it. "They always use the same old story. What else did they say? That the bomb might explode right here?"

"That's exactly what they said," said the old nun. She spoke abruptly, in snatches.

"He took one look at us three old women and obviously thought we'd be gullible enough to believe him," said the nun with green eyes, laughing. She too was feeling relieved. "Anyway, it wasn't so much what he said, as the way he said it. It was quite clear that they weren't going to let us near you. Luckily, you didn't need us."

"Saved by cigarettes," she joked.

"Cigarettes are very bad for you," said the large woman.

"What have you got in that suitcase?" said the old nun sharply. She was suspicious.

"Sister, please," chided her companion.

"No, it doesn't matter. I'd be happy to show you," she said, opening the suitcase on her knees and taking out the books. *Scarlet and Black* by Stendhal, *Quousque tandem* by Oteiza, the poems of Emily Dickinson, the anthology of Chinese poetry and the memoirs of Zavattini appeared on the table.

"You don't have to take out anything else. Sister Martina is convinced," said the nun with green eyes, picking up the memoirs of Zavattini.

"I didn't need convincing," said the old lady.

"Of course you didn't, sister."

The hostess came over with the coffee and had to make room for the tray. At that moment, however, the bus was going down a very bendy bit of the road and didn't allow for such balancing acts, and so she picked up the cup of coffee and indicated to the hostess that she should take the rest away.

She looked out of the window. Beneath the copper-coloured sky of Bilbao, the mountains were black, but it was a very sweet blackness.

"Just look what I've found here," the nun with green eyes exclaimed suddenly, as if startled. "Amazing!"

They all looked at her, including the hostess and the policeman with the red tie.

"Listen to this!" she said. She began reading a section from Zavattini's memoirs.

> While her daughter was ironing, Leroy's wife gave us a cup of coffee, all the time talking about Van Gogh as if he were one of the family. The wing of the building where Vincent used to live is almost in ruins; only a few madwomen live there now. The nuns . . .

The nun with green eyes stopped reading and looked around to make sure that they were all listening. Then, emphasizing each word, she read the sentence that had so startled her:

> The nuns referred to Vincent's paintings as "swallow-shit".

"Swallow-shit!" the nun exclaimed, opening her eyes very wide. "I can't believe it! Van Gogh's paintings swallow-shit!"

Irene took a sip of coffee. She didn't know what to think. The nun was probably trying to cheer her up, to entertain her by talking about things other than bombs and policemen.

"You modern nuns have so much more heart," said the large woman, emerging from the thoughts in which she had seemed to be immersed.

"That isn't why I read it out," said the nun. "I was just shocked to find those words the moment I opened the book.

But of course, the age we live in has a lot to do with it, we are all children of our time. That's how it was for the nuns who were working in the insane asylum where Van Gogh was staying. And we would react the same about certain things. Many of our mistakes are not properly speaking ours, they are the errors of the age we live in. But, forgive me, there I go sermonizing again."

"That's all right," she said, flicking her ash into the plastic cup. She had finished the coffee.

"What I meant was that we're not totally responsible for many of the things that we do, that the age we live in also plays its part."

"Thank you for that."

"I don't know why you were in prison, but I'm absolutely sure that it all belongs firmly in the past, and that you have no reason to return there. Those people," with a lift of her chin she indicated the area near the coffee machine, "have no right to pester you."

"That's what I think too. But they clearly don't agree."

She turned her head and looked behind her. The policeman who looked like a boxer and the one with the red tie were standing at the bottom of the stairs, talking. The hostess was doing her accounts.

"Look, I don't want to meddle in your affairs, but I'll just say one thing," said the nun, leaning towards her and lowering her voice. "I'm sure you've got a family and friends to rely on, but if you want to come to our house, you'd be more than welcome. No one will bother you and you might feel safe there. There's no shortage of work to do. Nobody gets bored."

"That's what I meant," said the large woman. "Nuns nowadays do a lot of good, they have more heart than they used to. Do you know what they do?"

She gave a knowing smile.

"No, I don't."

"I'll give you a clue. They could easily be wearing something that you yourself have on. And they would have more right than anyone to do so."

"Do get to the point!" said the old lady, looking bored.

"The red ribbon," said the large woman, ignoring the comment. "They look after people with AIDS. They share their lives with young AIDS patients. Admirable. Nobody wants to be bothered with sick people, whether it's AIDS they've got or something else. That's what society's like nowadays, it's awful. I myself . . . "

"You have no reason to complain," the nun with green eyes said, interrupting her and smiling. "You've told us all about your own illness and we know that now you're as right as rain."

"Where is the hospice?" she asked.

"About fifteen miles from the city, by the sea. It's a very beautiful place."

"But damp, very damp."

"On the one hand, I've no reason to complain, but on the other, I do," insisted the large woman, and before anyone could interrupt her, she launched into a litany of all the mistakes her doctors had made.

The window was covered with drops of rain. They were like diamonds: diamonds the size of a chickpea or a pea or a grain of rice or as tiny as the diamonds used by watchmakers.

She sat there looking at the drops, and the third dream of the journey began to take shape in her mind. But this time she was daydreaming, with only her imagination to help her.

Third Dream

She saw a beach, and on one side was a white house with blue windows, a villa built in the early part of the century in which – she learned this when her imagination allowed her to step inside – lived nine patients, five very young women and four very young men, all looking extremely depressed, and to help them there were four people, the nun with green eyes, the old nun, a male nurse and herself.

But what was she doing at the villa, apart from working as a nurse that is? At first, she couldn't understand what her mission was, but at last, after going into a room, the floor of which was scattered with cushions, she understood that she must be doing what Margarita had done in prison: consoling people, but consoling them with the marvellous words to be found in books, not with ordinary, off-the-cuff clichés. Then, so that the dream could progress, she imagined the room full of people, and she saw herself sitting amongst the patients, reading to them from a book. But what was she reading to them?

She searched her memory for some beautiful fragment, and she remembered a few lines that she had copied out in one of her notebooks. It was the end of the first poem that Margarita had taught them:

> Fight, my soul, for the hours and the moments;
> Each hour, each moment, can give you all;
> As when a captain rallies to the fight
> His scattered legions, and beats ruin back

> He, on the field, encamps, well pleased in mind.
> Yet surely him shall fortune overtake,
> Him smite in turn, headlong his musings drive;
> And that dear land, now safe, tomorrow fall.
> But he, unthinking, in the present good
> Solely delights, and all the camps rejoice.

She tried to examine the faces of the young men and women around her, and she had the feeling that, although they had liked the poem, they felt unable to imitate the captain and felt sadder than they had before the reading. Given their bleak future, it was best to cling to the present. But how did you do that? How could you grasp that particular nettle?

It seemed to her, in fact, that the poem and others like it could have a negative influence, since they named the insurmountable obstacle and brought it into the house, like a ghost, and her sole aim should be to create diversions, to cheer people up by whatever means possible. Why not use instead a collection of humorous poems? Poems like the one that used to make Antonia laugh so much:

> I always eat peas with honey,
> I've done it all my life,
> they do taste kind of funny,
> but it keeps them on the knife.

She saw at once that she had succeeded. Most of the young people were applauding and one of them was roaring with laughter, revealing a toothless mouth. Yes, that was the way forward. It wasn't a case of extolling happiness. You demonstrated happiness by making people happy.

She saw herself standing at the window of the room strewn with cushions, smoking a cigarette and looking out at the waves on the beach. Yes, she could stay in that house. It was a place set apart from the world, like the Pampas. Besides, she could be useful there.

The waves on the beach suddenly disappeared and she again saw the bus window speckled with rain. They had reached the final toll booth of the journey.

The large woman was still talking. The nun with green eyes was nodding, but she was looking at her.

"We're nearly there," said the nun, taking advantage of a pause in the conversation.

"I'll just smoke one last cigarette then," she said, looking out of the window. She saw the lights of a factory and the street-lamps in a deserted street. The rain was falling, forming threads, grey threads.

"I put the last one out myself. It was burning a hole in the plastic cup," said the large lady, trying to gain favour with the older nun. But the latter was still looking out of the window, taking no notice of her.

"You should start putting your things away in the suitcase. We're coming into Bilbao now," said the nun with green eyes.

The bus was going along a stretch of motorway from which you could see the whole city.

She peered out of the window. For miles around, the lights made everything look blurred, and it was impossible to see where the river was or where her house was in the old part of Bilbao.

The bus started heading downhill, then turned off up another street. She saw two men with umbrellas walking along the pavement, and further on, in an open space, a group of boys playing football. Bilbao. Her city.

She had to look away and concentrate on the cigarette she was smoking. She didn't want to get upset.

"It seems we're here," she heard someone say. The policeman

in the red tie had come over to her. "Please, ladies, don't look at me like that. I've just come to say goodbye. Anyway, I'm off duty now."

"You never give up, do you?" said the nun with green eyes.

"There are such a lot of tedious people in the world," said the old nun.

The policeman ignored them and addressed Irene instead.

"See you again, Irene. At least I hope so."

"I doubt that very much."

"I know I haven't behaved particularly well today, but I meant no harm by it. And I meant it when I said that I wanted to be your friend. You should at least give me a chance. I won't ask anything in return. Keep this, will you?"

Her jacket was still on one of the seats. The policeman picked it up and put his card in one of the pockets.

"My home phone number is on the card. I'm giving it to you in complete confidence, and I hope you'll respect that. As for you," he added, looking at the nun with green eyes, "I'd just like to say one thing."

"Well, make it short. We're nearly at the bus station," said the nun.

"It's very simple. You've been sitting around this table talking about people who are ill, people who are marginalized. Well, we're marginalized too, you know, especially here in the Basque country. We can't make friends, and we have to live in hiding, if we don't want some terrorist to kill us. That's why you were wrong to criticize our behaviour. We're just doing our job, whether we like it or not. Today, for example, I didn't like what I had to do. But we still had to do it. Now the job's done, and life goes on."

He was making a great effort to control himself and not to give way to his anger, but his face was flushed by the time he had finished his little speech. He seemed utterly sincere.

"I'll bear it in mind," said the nun.

"Home at last! And about time!" said the old nun, getting up. The bus had just driven into the bus station.

"Goodbye, Irene," said the policeman, holding out his hand to her.

"If we ever see each other again, then I'll shake your hand. But not now," she said, putting on her jacket.

There was a noise like a sneeze and the doors sprang open. The passengers from the upper deck started to come down the stairs.

"All right, Irene, see you then," said the policeman. He joined his colleague with the flattened nose, and the two of them got off the bus.

"We're going to get a taxi. What about you?" asked the nun with green eyes. After what they had talked about downstairs, the question was an invitation for her to accompany them.

She decided to consider that possibility. She could try it, just for a couple of weeks, until she saw how the land lay in Bilbao. Why not? She could go there tonight. She would call her father and tell him that she needed to be somewhere quiet for a while, not for any particular reason, just as a precaution.

She got off the bus and looked around. Where were the policemen? Would they follow her? From that point of view too, it seemed a good idea to go with the nuns. They were her insurance policy.

"I need to get a taxi as well. I live really close, but I feel too weak to walk," said the large woman.

"I'll go with you as far as the taxis," she said.

It was about twenty yards from the door of the bus to the taxi rank, but that distance seemed much longer, because it was like a descent into reality. With each step she took, the beachside villa for the sick seemed farther off, and her plan to go there and work as a nurse or assistant seemed more and more unreal. In the end, when they reached the taxi, her plan – like all chimeras, like all dreams – had vanished into thin air. No, she wouldn't accept the invitation, she wouldn't go and take care of those young patients in order to assure herself of a refuge where she could live apart from the world. Besides, there was no running away. Like the very air itself, the malignant substances of this world penetrated every crack, impregnating everything, even the lives of people who shut themselves up in watertight rooms.

"I think I'll walk. My family lives just over there, in the old part," she said to the nun with green eyes.

"That sounds like a good idea, but don't forget us. Drop by whenever you like," she said, handing her a card.

"I will," she said, taking the card and putting it in her jacket pocket.

"We're going to get wet if we stand here much longer," said the old woman, pointing up at the rain.

"Goodbye then. See you."

The walk to the old part of the city was another descent, but this time her steps were crossing not the space between dream and reality, but another simpler space separating outside from inside. She had been away for a long time and now she was going home. When she reached the bridge over the river and saw all the places she had known as a child – the Arenal Park, the church of San Nicolás, the Arriaga Theatre – she began to feel what Margarita had said she would feel when she left prison, that the things from her past life would start to speak to her, be it the stones the buildings were made of or the boats on the river or the signs over the cafés – "Welcome, welcome home" – and that those welcoming voices would give her strength.

Before she got to the other end of the bridge, she stopped and looked up at the sky. It wasn't entirely overcast. Despite the drizzle, she could just see the moon between two clouds.

The translator would like to thank Bernardo Atxaga,
Annella McDermott, Antonio Martín and Ben Sherriff
for all their help and advice.

Poems, songs and prose extracts quoted in the novel

"Beat at the bars" from "Bars" by Carl Sandburg

"I never saw a wild thing sorry for itself" from "Self-pity" by
D. H. Lawrence

"No, people never like those who keep their own faith" from *La
mauvaise réputation* by Georges Brassens

"I like my women" from *Me gustan las mujeres* by José de Espronceda

"The mind of an ex-prisoner" from *El ánimo de quien ha estado preso*
by Joseba Sarrionandia

"If you want to write to me" from a popular Spanish song

"Dalle più alte stelle" by Michelangelo

"Solomon Grundy" a popular children's rhyme

"When I was a child in Orio" from *Quousque tandem* by Jorge Oteiza

"As the sun set" from *Scarlet and Black* by Stendhal

"Though far apart" from "The two hearts", a traditional Chinese
poem

"Last night I dreamt" from a song by The Smiths

"The grass so little has to do" by Emily Dickinson

"O Venus, evening star" by Sappho

"Goodnight Irene" popular song from the United States

"Ixil ixilik dago" popular Basque song

"Little Lamb, who made thee?" from "The Lamb" by William Blake

"Aboard a train of oblivion" from "Run Run se fue p'al Norte" by
Violeta Parra

"The whole of it came not at once" by Emily Dickinson

"While her daughter was ironing" from *Diario di cinema e di vita* by
Cesare Zavattini

"Fight, my soul, for the hours and the moments" from "Not yet, my
soul" by Robert Louis Stevenson

"I always eat peas with honey" an anonymous rhyme

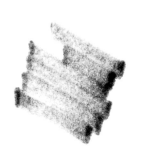